LOVE, TEMPEST, AND WAR

Best wishes.
Sincerely,
Meredith Forgey

LOVE, TEMPEST, AND WAR

A World War II Love Story

A Novel by

MERRITT YORGEY

Passer Books and Publishing Co.
Coopersburg, PA 18036

Library of Congress Catalog Card Number: 90-70782

ISBN 0-9626569-0-9

Text design by Ted Schick, Jr.
Cover Illustration by Derek Buckner

Printed in the United States of America.

To my wife, Helen,
and
to my children, Carole, James, and Donald,
and
to Ludwig F. Schlecht, Jr. and Theodore W. Schick, Jr. of
the Philosophy Department, Muhlenberg College, for their
generous guidance and counsel.

"The care of the universal happiness of all rational beings is the business of God and not of man...to man is allotted...the care of his own happiness, and that of his family, his friends, and his country."

--Adam Smith

Table of Contents

ONE

A Devastating Letter

Many things on earth must await the passing of time before they can come into existence and have their being. The oak tree from an acorn, the human fetus, a forest fire, a spewing volcano, a budding flower, all were latent forces, smoldering, straining to become, developing, constrained, yet destined to spring forth into their ultimate potential form.

A human life is like that, a man's life or a woman's life. Martin Miller's life was like that. He was twenty-two years old when his latent potential began to unfurl.

For several weeks Martin had been waiting for a letter from Alice. It was frustrating, disappointing and even embarrassing as each mail call passed without that letter from Alice; and then, when it finally arrived and he had read it, he erupted with a seething, "Damn her!" He couldn't believe his eyes. His throat tightened as he shrieked, "Damn her, damn her, damn her."

"What's wrong with you?" yelled one of his shipmates who was standing near him on the main deck.

Martin didn't answer. He took the letter, crumbled it into one of his large hands and jammed it into the palm of the other, and then put it as a crumbled up ball into his dungaree pocket. He had to do something. He walked swiftly from the fantail, along the main deck, to the bow of the ship and then back down the other side. He took a long drink of cold water, at the cooler near the mess hall. Back on the fantail, on the starboard side, the workout punching bag was in place in its permanent rack. Spotting it, Martin walked over and started working out on it. He hit hard, harder than he had ever hit it before. Then he steadily increased the tempo of the rhythm, hitting harder and harder, faster and faster until the rack vibrated in harmony and transmitted its frequency throughout the adjacent structural steel of the ship.

Soon a crowd of his shipmates gathered around him and watched, fascinated and bewildered.

"The guy's crazy," said one of the onlookers.

Scott Ackermun came by, watched him for a few moments, then saw that there were tears streaming down Martin's face. He went over, put his hand on his friend's shoulder and stopped him.

"Do you wanna tell me what's botherin' ya?" he asked.

Martin reached into his pocket, took out the crumbled letter and crammed it into Scotty's hand. The onlookers left. Scotty smoothed out the letter and began to read:

September 10, 1941

Dear Martin,

I hardly know how to begin this letter. As you know I went to summer school at the University in Chicago to take a couple of required courses which I had continually put off because I wasn't sure I was going to need them. My student advisor recommended taking them so I'd qualify to complete my work for a masters in psychology. Well, to get to the point, you remember my psychology instructor, Prof. Charles Smith. He transferred to Chicago and since psychology is my major, I was very much interested in keeping in touch with him because he could help me with my studies and he was somebody I knew fairly well from back home. But then as weekend after weekend dragged on without being with you, I got very lonely. Charles helped to fill those lonely hours. He knows so much about the subjects I am interested in and I learned a lot from him. We never went anywhere alone at first. We always met at the library or the college shop or on campus somewhere. We had wonderful long talks.

Then one afternoon it was rainy and miserable. We had been downtown to the public library. Afterwards, when we went out and saw what the weather was like, Charles said he lived only a short distance away and he invited me to go along to his place. The weather was miserable, so I went with him.

I never thought about what his place would be like. But it was a beautiful little apartment, in one of those tall apartment buildings. It was a new experience and I enjoyed it. Charles suggested I try my hand at cooking up a little meal. He had plenty of food in the refrigerator, everything, and it was such a cute, convenient, little kitchen. Well, of course, you know I can cook. It's impossible for a girl to grow up in a Pennsylvania German family without learning to cook. So, I really enjoyed it.

But before I had the meal prepared and on the table, Charles brought in a bottle of wine, which we had with the appetizer. After we ate we had some more wine. I was feeling just wonderful. I walked over to the window and looked down to the street many floors below. It was still rainy and windy and miserable outside, while inside it was so cozy and secure. The people looked so small down there on the street as they went scurrying back and forth, trying to keep from getting wet. Then I saw a sailor holding an umbrella for his girl and the wind caught the umbrella and blew it away from them. They dashed into a

*store doorway. The sailor seemed to be trying to shield his girl
from the rain. Then I thought of you and I wished that you were
there with me. I felt sad. Charles must have noticed it. He came
over to me and put his arm around my waist.*

*He said: "What's the matter, Allie?" He said "Allie" the
way you used to say "Allie."*

"Oh, just daydreaming," I said. "It's an old habit of mine."

*We sat on the sofa and we talked for a long time, and he
helped me to untangle some confusing thoughts which have been
bothering me for a long time. He convinced me that all those inhibitions that I had, and you have, about love and sex are really
wrong. They are based on false ideas and false ideals.*

*Our parents misled us. But can we put all of the blame on
them? They too were misled by their parents, and they got their
false notions from their ancestors, and on and on. Our knowledge of sex comes to us steeped in mystery and ignorance.*

*Our ancestors were so scared of getting pregnant, and they
had no way of preventing it, that even the church taught that
sex, except under certain conditions, was evil. So our parents
also believed it was evil and they wouldn't even talk to us about
it.*

*They left us with a sense of guilt and shame about everything
concerning love and sex and reproduction, and millions of people
appear upon the earth and leave it again without ever knowing
what joy and fulfillment there is in uninhibited love and sex.*

*Charles thinks somewhere, somehow this chain of ignorance
must come to an end.*

*Well, when the truth of all this finally got through to me,
when it finally sank in, it was like being released, freed from cap-
tivity. It was exhilarating, and when Charles put his arms
around me, I wanted to make love with him, and we did. We
made love in ways that I had often dreamed of making love with*

you. He caressed every inch of me with his hands and his lips and his eyes; and I returned it, caress for caress, kiss for kiss, just the way my whole body had often cried out with desire for you, and I'm truly sorry that I was never able to tell you that.

Charles and I are going to be married as soon as we can make the arrangements. This letter may sound morbid and in-decent and cruel to you, Martin. I thought it out thoroughly before de-ciding how to tell you. And I could have done it differently. But I know how eagerly, how desperately you want to learn the truth about life. I know how sincere you were when you thought that by becoming a minister you would learn the truth, and how convinced you were when you gave that up and joined the Navy. That's why I am writing to you in so much detail . . . This is life. This is truth, at least it is part of the truth you so eagerly seek. This is the way it has been for a long time. It is the way it will probably always be.

There was a time when I thought there could only be one per-son in the whole world that I could really love. I thought that was you. I probably still love you just as much as I always have, but I love Charles just as much as I love you. I also know that there are other men in the world I could love just as well, and it is the same for you, Martin, and everyone. Each of us must find someone we love, someone we like, someone we communicate with, and then go about the business of living, as God intended us to live--to love God, to love our neighbors, to love one another, to bear the next generation and to pass on to them the knowledge of life as we understand it.

Good luck to you, Martin. Keep right on looking for the truth in your own way. It is the only way you will find it.

Sincerely,

Alice

P.S. I'm sending the ring back to your home by insured mail.

When Scotty finished reading the letter, Martin took it and re-read it again and was finally convinced that it was not some trick of his imagination.

"I'll just have to accept the fact that it is true," he said aloud, to himself. "And to think that only four months ago she...Oh, Alice, why did you do this to me? How can I answer a letter such as this? There is no answer."

Scotty walked away, unable to offer any solace. Martin lay back on a large hatch cover and closed his eyes. He dozed off for a few minutes, and he was awakened abruptly by the stinging words of the Boatswain's Mate, Jim Johnson, shouting, "Wake up there, lover-boy. Come on, let's turn to. We got no time in this man's Navy for love-sick sailors."

Martin sat up quickly, but knowing in that instant he was fed up with this kind of harassment from Jim Johnson, he stood up, stretched his six foot to its fullest, and looked directly into his eyes. He held the stare for a long minute, not saying a word. Johnson looked right back at him, also without uttering a word.

"What's wrong, lover-boy, are you mad or something?" Johnson said, finally, to break the confrontation.

Martin felt the anger crawling up inside him with each heart beat. The blood rushed to his neck and face as he tried to stifle his anger and embarrassment. For the past several weeks he had become better acquainted with men of various ranks and rates on board the ship, both enlisted men and officers. He tried several times with different approaches, but for some reason or other, which he could not understand, he could not get even one friendly word from Jim Johnson. He wondered what it was that caused Johnson to be so antagonistic. He felt like smashing that arrogant, repulsive face. But he heard his mother's voice ringing in his ears, saying, "If thine enemy smite thee on the right cheek, turn to him the other also."

But he could also hear his father's response to that voice, saying, "That's bull-oney!"

Finally, letting down his guard and turning aside, he said: "I don't have the duty this afternoon. I have liberty today and I'm going ashore." He said it defiantly.

"Well, O. K.," Jim Johnson answered. "Then get your ass out of here."

TWO

A Sailor on the Rebound

Norfolk, Virginia, was just like any other town Martin had visited, he observed, as he walked along Granby street, except that it had more bars and cafes. Scotty had the 0800 to 1200 duty and couldn't make the first liberty party, so this was Martin's first liberty ashore without his friend since he had been assigned to the ship.

The liberty party dispersed into singles, pairs and groups of three, and some of the men rushed into the first bar they could find, while others stopped at some of the numerous amusement spots and stores along the main street. Martin was depressed, and angry. He wanted to be alone. He stepped into one of the barrooms, deciding that maybe Scotty's advice was best after all. "Go get yourself a few good drinks, get drunk and you'll be able to forget all about it, then you'll feel better."

After several drinks, however, his anger turned into rage. He decided he was going to call Alice, no matter what it cost. Maybe he could talk her out of marrying that damn jerk, that psychology professor! He knew he had disappointed her by joining the Navy, but he didn't think she would go this far, so soon. But his rage was soon absorbed by the self doubt of rejection, then remorse and regret. He truly loved Alice Schneider. He decided to get a room in a hotel where he could collect his thoughts and then talk to her on the telephone in private. Afterwards, hopefully, he would get a good night's sleep in a real bed.

He stood at the bar because there were no empty stools. He looked around for an empty table or a booth, and as he surveyed the room, he spotted Jim Johnson with a girl seated next to him in one of the booths. Another seaman sat across from them. On impulse, before leaving to find a hotel room, Martin decided to walk over to Johnson's booth and make one more attempt to extend the hand of friendship. Although he was not sure of his own motives, for he had been extremely angry with him for the humiliation he had suffered at his hand, it bothered him that he had not been able to develop at least one civil conversation with Johnson. This was the man with whom he would have to work closely every day.

"Hi, Jim Johnson," he said, as he approached the booth. He put on his best, most friendly smile. "This must be a good place if you come here."

Johnson looked at him through blurry eyes. His drinks had apparently already taken effect. "Well, look who's here. It's lover-boy Miller. Hell, no, Miller, this is a real crumby joint. That's what this place is. My friend Lundy here, this is his favorite joint. But Cathy here, and me, we've got better places than this we go to. Right, Cathy?"

The girl looked at Martin. "Right," she said, smiling.

"This is my favorite woman, Cathy. Cathy, this here's one of the new 'boots' that came aboard the other week, I told you about, remember? This here's Miller, one of my new deck hands."

"Hi, Cathy, nice to meet you," Martin said.

"Hello," she answered.

Johnson tilted up his beer mug and took a long drink. "Let's have another beer," he said. "How about you, Loverboy?"

"I was drinking scotch and soda, thanks."

"Scotch and soda! What the hell are ya doing drinkin' that fancy stuff? Have a beer." He summoned the waitress and ordered four mugs of beer.

"You might as well sit in with us," Cathy said. "He's going to insist you have the beer he's ordered."

"Yeah, Miller, sit down and have a beer with us. Don't be so hard to get along with," Johnson said. It was obvious he had had too much to drink.

"I'm not trying to be hard to get along with," Martin said, as he sat down alongside Lundy. "I stopped by your booth to be friendly."

Someone dropped money in the juke box and several couples started dancing in front of it. The music seemed much too loud for the size of the room. The waitress arrived with the beer. Then Johnson raised his mug and toasted with, "Here's mud in your eye." Whatever that meant, Martin did not know. So he lifted his glass and offered, "To your health." He took several large swallows. The beer tasted good. He hadn't had any beer for a long time.

After the second beer, on which Johnson had insisted, he said to Martin, "Hey, look, Lundy and I have some business to do down the street. We'll be back in about half an hour. You could stay here and keep an eye on Cathy. Don't let any of those wolves at the bar get to her. O. K.? And don't run off with her yourself, either. Ya hear?"

"Sure, sure," Martin said. "I'll look after her, no problem."

Johnson picked up a duffel bag from under the seat and then he and Lundy left.

When they were gone, Martin leaned back in his seat and looked at Cathy directly for the first time. She smiled. "My full name is Martin Miller," he said. "What's yours?"

"I'm Catherine Welsh," she answered forthrightly, and seemed to be saying, "and I'm proud of it."

Martin's pulse quickened, and suddenly he realized he was doing something he hadn't done for many years, not since he had met Alice. He was trying to become better acquainted with a new girl, a stranger, and he was trying to make a good impression. He began to feel the excitement of it. Cathy was not a raving beauty, but she was easy to look at. She had the soft femininity he expected to see in a southern girl. Her soft voice and accent would not let her deny being southern. She had the kindness, the warmth, and the hospitable approach to strangers of a refined Southerner.

The waitress came to the booth and Cathy said, "Yes, thank you, I'll have another." Martin ordered for them.

"I'm from Pennsylvania," he said, trying to make conversation. "Where's your home?"

"Well, I've been living up here for several years, since I graduated from high school. My Daddy is a civilian employee at the Portsmouth Navy Yard. But we are originally from North Carolina -- Winston-Salem," Cathy answered.

It was pleasant sitting there talking with this new acquaintance. She was a very pleasant person. He wondered what she was doing with a guy like Johnson. The drinks had relaxed him completely and his mood had also changed.

"Where did you meet Jim Johnson, if you don't mind my asking?"

"Oh, that's all right," she said in her southern drawl. "Actually, Jim is from my home town. We went to the same high school. Then I hadn't seen him for several years until his ship made Norfolk its home port about a year ago. He looked me up and I have dated him a number of times since."

The juke box was playing "Blue Moon," with Bing Crosby singing.

"Would you like to dance?" Martin asked.

"Oh, I don't know, Jim doesn't like me to dance with others when we're on a date. I guess it's because he doesn't dance much himself."

"Do you like to dance?"

"Oh, yes. I love to dance."

"Then, let's dance." He got up and reached for her hand. She immediately followed him over to the juke box, and they danced to the end of "Blue Moon." They danced to several more numbers. Time passed swiftly. Martin thought how great it was to have a girl in his arms again. Cathy was a tall girl, taller than he had guessed while she was sitting. She had long legs, and she was slender. But the softness of her body against his, while they danced, quickly aroused him. He hadn't realized until now how much he missed the company of a woman. He desperately missed Alice.

"We'd better sit down," Martin said.

"Yeah," Cathy answered. She was perspiring.

They hadn't noticed while they were dancing that Johnson, and his friend, had returned, and was waiting for them. "What the hell are you two up to?" he shouted. He was more intoxicated now than he had been when he left.

Cathy responded with an embarrassed, "Nothing."

"Nothing your ass," Johnson shouted, attracting the attention of other patrons.

"Look, Johnson, we were only dancing, nothing else," Martin said, becoming more angry with Johnson's bad manners and foul language than with his accusations.

"Dancing your ass," Johnson said. "I saw you practically dry-jazzing her right there on the dance floor."

"Jim!" Cathy now shouted. "If you don't shut up, I'll leave, and I'll never see you again!"

"Aw, shut up yourself," Johnson responded.

"O. K., then," Cathy said, turning white with anger. She turned to Martin and said, "Would you mind taking me down to the Portsmouth ferry? I can make it home from there."

Martin hardly had any other choice, so he went with her as she started out of the tavern.

They walked in silence down Granby street, then through the City Arcade to the river. Martin waited with her until the Portsmouth Ferry arrived. "I'm sorry about the way things turned out," he said, finally.

"No, you don't have to feel that way. This sort of thing has happened before and I told Jim the last time that I wasn't going to stand for it anymore. He gets that way when he drinks and he usually drinks when he comes ashore. If it hadn't been you, it would've been someone else. Thanks for coming down here to the ferry with me. I'll have to go now. Good bye." She held out her hand. He took it, and momentarily he thought about asking to see her again, but then had second thoughts about it. That would only further antagonize Johnson. But, wait a minute, he thought, she's a nice person. He asked for her address; "So I can drop you a note and let you know how things are going." She gave it willingly. He wrote it on a card he had in his wallet.

"Good-bye, Cathy," he said. "It was nice meeting you. Good luck to you." It was strange, he thought, how he hated saying good-bye to people he liked.

THREE

Violence and Another Man's Woman

After the ferry left, he walked back up Granby street and checked a couple of hotels for a room. He finally got one at the Monticello. Then, as soon as he had checked in, he picked up the telephone and placed his call to Alice in Chicago. After considerable delay, the operator advised that Charles Smith at the address he had given had a private listing. He then tried Alice's number on campus but this number was no longer in service.

Frustrated, he laid across the bed, intending to rest for a few minutes and then go out for something to eat. But it would be depressing, he thought, to be alone, here in this strange port town, for the rest of the day and the night, in a hotel room. His thoughts drifted back to Cathy. He thought of dancing with her at the tavern and of walking her to the ferry. Impulsively he reached for his wallet and pulled out the card with her address and telephone number. He picked up the telephone again and dialed. A man answered, her father, Martin assumed. He asked for Cathy.

"Hello," she said.

"This is Martin Miller. Remember?"

"Oh, yes, Martin. But I didn't expect to hear from you so soon."

"I know this may be a little out of line, but I'm alone and I don't know anyone here. I was wondering if you would join me for dinner and maybe a movie."

"Well, I don't know," Cathy answered slowly.

"I understand that they have a very good dining room here at the Monticello, where I'm staying, and dinner music, and dancing later."

"You're staying at the Monticello?"

"Yes."

"Aw, hold on a minute, let me ask my Daddy if he'll take me back to the ferry. Then we could meet where you walked me to this afternoon."

After a long delay she returned to the telephone. "Excuse the delay, but it's all right. I had to explain to my father how I met you. He's not too crazy about me going out with sailors. But it's all right. I'll meet you at the ferry, on the Norfolk side, at seven thirty."

"Fine," Martin said. "I'll see you there."

He took a short nap, showered and shaved, and then left the hotel, leaving plenty of time to walk to the ferry.

When they returned to the Monticello, they were seated at a very cozy table in a corner of the dining room. They dined leisurely. The service was elegant old south, with the finest china and silverware, and elegant, old black waiters. They had cocktails to start, and they had wine with dinner. They relaxed. They lingered. They talked. They enjoyed one another's company to the fullest. Time slipped away as they engaged in the small talk of an evolving friendship. They talked about food and drink and movies and school and college, and they shared information about their families, and finally, with his tongue lubricated by the alcohol they had consumed, he talked about Alice Schneider, and about her letter.

Later they danced to the music of a big band, and while they danced they talked some more. "I feel lucky that I met you at this time. I was depressed, down in the dumps, as we say back home, so I really do appreciate your accepting my invitation."

"I'd say you are sort of on the rebound," Cathy said. "And one of my girl friends warned me to be careful with a guy who's on the rebound."

"Well, I don't think I'm on the rebound just yet, that will be a new experience for me," Martin said. "but you don't have to worry about me. I'm just happy to have your company and 'your ear.' It's too bad that you're Jim Johnson's girlfriend or I would probably try to see you again, more often."

"I'm not Jim Johnson's girlfriend. I'm not even his date any more," Cathy snapped. "I meant it when I told him I wouldn't see him anymore. But you will have to learn something about being in the Navy, especially if you're assigned to duty aboard a ship. It's difficult to have a normal, steady relationship with a sailor who is serving on a ship. You'll be going to sea, soon, no doubt, and then who knows if and when we'll see one another again. I know how it is. That's why I haven't found a steady boyfriend. Everyone around here is connected with the Navy, and nothing is ever permanent."

This thought had an unexpected effect upon Martin's alcohol-saturated mind. "Let's leave now and go up to my room," he blurted out suddenly, forcefully.

"Oh, no. I couldn't do that," Cathy responded immediately.

"Why not?"

"Because you're a sailor," Cathy said, with a knowing smile. "But, I have a better idea. It's getting late. Let's go back to my house. We can sit and talk. My parents and my little sister go to bed early."

They walked back to the ferry, and in Portsmouth took a taxi to her home, a two-story, white frame house, in the heart of an all white, residential neighborhood. They sat on the wooden swing on the front porch for a short time and then went into the living room. The lights were turned low, and all was quiet in the house. They sat closely together, on the sofa, and they too were quiet.

Martin felt the same strong attraction for Cathy that he had felt earlier while they were dancing, in front of the juke box, at the tavern where they first met. It was a feeling of want, of needing, not of lust, he thought, but an indescribable hunger, emanating from deep within his being.

"I want you, Cathy," Martin whispered into her ear.

There was a long silence. Then finally, "You really work fast," she said. "It's not that I . . . but . . . we just can't. I just couldn't do that. It's our first date, for Heaven's sake," Cathy whispered.

"I'm sorry," Martin whispered, "but all of a sudden I thought, what a shame it would be if we never see one another again. Now you probably think that's all I had in mind when I called you."

"Oh, no, I know you're sincere. But it just wouldn't be right. It would be awfully, awfully wrong. We simply don't know each other well enough. I think you know that, don't you?"

"Yes, of course I know, and I respect your proper response to an improper advance. It's a good thing women are stronger than men in that department."

"I'm not so sure we are," Cathy said, as she snuggled into his arms.

But, suddenly, out of the quietness, there was a loud, unsteady knocking at the door. They were both startled. Cathy quickly jumped up off of the sofa and tidied herself. She went to the door and asked, "Who is it?"

"It's me, Jim Johnson," came the reply.

"What do you want?"

"Open up, I want to talk to you," Johnson said, as he pounded loudly on the door.

In order to keep him quiet, Cathy partly opened the door. Jim started to push it open further, and in that instant he caught sight of Martin. "What the hell is that 'boot' doing here?" he shouted. "Miller, you sneaky son-of-a-bitch. I figured I couldn't trust you. I introduce you to my girlfriend, and you move in like an old cock-master." He pushed his way past Cathy into the room, and lunged toward Martin. Martin quickly jumped up off of the sofa to defend himself. Johnson was drunk, very drunk. He was loud and grew louder. So loud that the disturbance awoke Cathy's father, who came down the stairs.

"What's going on here?" Mr. Welsh demanded. He recognized Johnson. "Jim, Cathy told me about the incident this afternoon, and I agree with her one hundred percent. Now, you're drunk and disorderly. So you just leave this house at once."

"I just came to esplain to Cathy," he slurred, "and then I find this freakin' Miller here. I'm gonna break his God damn neck."

"You get out of here immediately, do you hear?" Welsh roared.

He grabbed Johnson by the arm and shoved him toward the door. Martin moved in angrily and grabbed Johnson's other arm, and together they got him out of the door, off of the porch and onto the street. Johnson apparently knew he was overpowered. He looked Martin directly in the eye.

"I'm gonna get you for this, you shithead," he said. Then he left, cursing as he went down the street.

Back inside it was an embarrassing situation. But Cathy quickly recovered and introduced Martin to her father.

"This is an unusual way to meet," Welsh said. "But I never did like that Johnson, even if he is from back home. Anybody that gets mean like that when they drink is a bad person. Cathy, you'd better learn that."

"I'm sorry about all this, Mr. Welsh," Martin said. "I guess it's mostly my fault."

"Well, it's too late to discuss it now. I'm going back to bed. It's late, and you two better be calling it a night too."

"Yes, Daddy," Cathy answered. "But Martin will have to stay a little while. I don't want him to have to go back on the same ferry with Jim Johnson."

"Yeah, I see what you mean. Very well, good night," he said as he went back upstairs.

Martin and Cathy sat back down on the sofa. They sat for a long time in silence, holding hands. Finally, Cathy said, "Will you still write to me and let me know how things are going? You still have my address, right?"

"Yes, I sure will," he said, as he got up to leave. At the door he kissed her passionately. She clung to him as if she would never let him go. But he pulled away and left, and he was overwhelmed by a deep sense of loss. Oh, how I hate leaving people that I like, he thought.

As he walked down Granby Street again on the way back to the hotel he noticed one of those white-fronted restaurants across the street. He decided to go there for a cup of coffee and something to eat before turning in. It was early in the morning. As he was about to cross the street a taxicab crossed in front of him. In the back seat were several sailors and girls. They looked haggard, sleepy-eyed and unkempt. He waited for the taxi to pass and wondered at what a night they must have had, then crossed the street and entered the little white-fronted restaurant.

Inside there were about a half dozen sailors, several of them drunk and boisterous. They were no doubt stopping for black coffee and food to help sober them up before returning to their ships. Martin sat at the counter and ordered eggs, bacon and home fries. Several stools away there were two sailors arguing and getting louder by the minute.

"I could've had her myself," said one of them. He was the shorter of the two and he had a broad face and large ears.

"Aw, the hell you could of. She had her eye on me," said the other. He was tall and hefty.

Martin took a second look and recognized them. It was Jim Johnson and his friend, Lundy, from the tavern. Johnson looked up at that very moment and saw Martin. "Well look who the hell is here." He shoved himself away from the counter, walked up to Martin and slapped him hard on the back. Martin's coffee cup flew out of his hand and the coffee splattered all over him. His anger flared up quickly the moment the coffee hit him, and the anger put him on the offensive. Quick as a flash he grabbed hold of Johnson and shoved him backwards. He'd had enough of this big jerk, he thought, he wasn't going to put up with any more of his bull.

But the instant he did this, Lundy, the short one, realizing he had a new antagonist, yelled: "Get your dirty hands offa my buddy." And in another instant both of them pounced upon Martin like wild beasts. Martin instinctively defended himself. As much as he normally disliked violence, he now felt a surge of real satisfaction travelling like an electric current through his entire body, as he matched them blow for blow. All of the pent up frustration brought about by Alice's letter and the suppressed anger over Jim Johnson's treatment of him, and of Cathy, finally found an outlet.

"Revenge is mine, saith the Lord," Martin muttered under his breath, "but tonight, revenge is mine." He glared at Johnson, who had stepped in and landed several blows to Martin's stomach. Martin lashed out with repeated deadly lefts and rights to Johnson's head. Johnson swung wildly, and then with a strange look on his face, he slumped to the floor like a wet rag. Then, just as Lundy stepped in again, Martin's eyes shifted momentarily and he saw shore patrolmen running up the street toward the restaurant, their police whistles shrilling loudly. In that moment of distracted attention, Lundy caught Martin squarely on the nose with a sledgehammer fist. He could feel his own warm blood spatter all over his face.

As the shore patrolmen entered the restaurant most of the others present quieted down quickly and assumed an attitude of indifference. There was no mistake as to who the offenders were, however, and the SP's lost no time in herding them through the door after Johnson's friend got him back on his feet.

Martin tried to explain: "I was minding my own business, when ..."

"Shut up," yelled one of the SP's, waving his night stick and looking into Martin's blood spattered face. "You sure don't look like you were minding your own business!"

About a block down the street one of the SP's went into a phone booth, evidently to call Shore Patrol Headquarters. The other one stood by to guard the prisoners. Lundy was standing alongside and slightly behind this remaining shore patrolman. Without warning he swung around and slammed the SP on the side of the head, knocking the unsuspecting victim to his knees. Then he dashed off down the street like a scared rabbit. Johnson, bleary-eyed and only half conscious, yelled, "Oh, shit," and then slumped to the pavement again. The injured SP, recovering in an instant and acting instinctively, regained his feet and rushed after the fleeing Lundy, forgetting he had two other prisoners.

Sizing up the situation quickly, Martin saw that this was an opportunity to get away. He took one quick look at Johnson squirming on the pavement. He had mixed emotions about whether to stay and help him or flee. Terror seized him and he took off down the street in the opposite direction, running for all he was worth. He ran the block in record time, then darted into an alley. He rounded the corner into another alley, then out on another street at the side entrance of the hotel. There were only a few people in the lobby. He got out his handkerchief and held it over his nose and mouth. At the desk he could hear the click, click

of a typewriter. Martin slowed down, walked past the
desk casually with his face turned away from the direction
of the desk. He held his breath as he waited for the
elevator. When the elevator opened, he slipped in
sideways past the sleepy operator and mumbled, "five."

When he got into his room, he quickly soaked a towel
with cold water, doused his face and head and put a com-
press on his nose to stop the bleeding. A quick examina-
tion showed him there was nothing broken, just a cut lip
and a very sore, bleeding nose.

"My God, all that happened so fast," he said aloud. "I
don't believe it." Then he showered and laid back down on
the bed to get some more rest before heading back to the
ship.

FOUR

Death, Involvement, and Dilemma

As he walked in through the main gate of the Norfolk Naval Base Martin was aware of the frantic activity taking place on the docks. All this activity was probably due to the fact that German U-boats were active again in the Atlantic, he thought. They might attack United States ships at any moment and force the U.S. into war, and the U. S. Navy was apparently bound and determined to be ready.

Martin hurriedly strode along the piers, taking in as much of the activity as his fast pace allowed. Panting harbor tugs moved huge merchants ships into place at their berths on the long piers. Fog horns blared intermittently in gruff voices that contrasted with the rapid toots of the little tugs, while the shouting of deck officers and the shrill sounds of the boatswain's whistle came garbled through the fog-laden air. Merchant ships and Navy ships, battleships, cruisers and destroyers were anchored everywhere nearby in the Chesapeake Bay or tied to the piers, taking on stores.

He made it back aboard his ship in time to change into dungarees and get to the mess hall for breakfast. In the mess hall he saw Scotty Ackermun at one of the tables with a cup of coffee. Martin got his tray of food and joined him. He had forgotten momentarily about his sore face, and on the first spoonful of corn flakes he shook his head in agony.

Scotty looked at him, bewildered. "What happened to you? Your face looks a little out of shape."

"I'll tell you later," Martin answered, as he got up from the table.

"Did you hear we shove off in the morning for the Brooklyn Navy Yard?"

"I guess it is about time," Martin answered as they hurried aft to report for work detail.

Later, without any fanfare, the loudspeakers vibrated with the Captain's husky voice: "Now hear this. This is the Captain. It is, with sadness, that I must announce the death of Boatswain's Mate First Class, James P. Johnson. He was pronounced dead on arrival at the Norfolk Naval Hospital. The cause of his death has not as yet been determined. Repeat. Jim Johnson, Boatswain's Mate First Class was pronounced dead on arrival early this morning at the Norfolk Naval Hospital. All hands will observe a moment of silence as the Chief Boatswain sounds taps."

Immediately all activity on board ceased and the ship's officers and crew stood with bowed heads in shocked silence as the Chief piped the mournful taps.

Martin had noticed that Jim Johnson hadn't made it back on board, and he'd had some anxious thoughts wondering what had become of him. But when he heard the Captain's announcement he literally went into shock! Jim Johnson dead! No! That can not be! It was he, Martin Miller, who out of anger, resentment and the desire for revenge, lashed out at Jim Johnson. Oh yes, he was relieving his anger and frustration and was getting revenge for the rotten treatment he received from Johnson. But he didn't want to kill him! Had those blows killed him? No! No! He could not have killed him. He could not kill anything. No such thought ever crossed his mind or invaded his dreams. No, he couldn't even kill a rat. He remembered the baby rats he once tried to destroy, to get rid of the pests in the carriage shed behind the house. How he threw up and almost failed to finish the job because he could not stand to see anything die. But Jim Johnson was dead! How could this be? It's the sixth or seventh commandment, 'Thou shalt not kill!' My God, how could this have happened, he muttered, almost incoherently.

Scotty saw the agony on Martin's face. "What happened last night?"

"I got into a fight with Jim Johnson and another sailor. The SP's picked us up, but we got away," Martin answered, and with terror in his voice, related the other details of the incident.

"Oh, shoot," Scotty said under his breath. He fell silent. Then finally asked, "Was the other sailor from our ship?"

"No. He wasn't one of our crew."

"Then let me tell you something, Mart, something very important. I know this man's Navy. Whatever you do, don't tell nobody, not a soul, what happened. Don't volunteer any information to nobody. There ain't nobody else who could connect you with Johnson's death, except maybe one of them SP's and that ain't likely. Don't say a word. If you say you know something about it, they'll hang you with it sure as hell."

"But, look, Scotty, I . . ."

"Don't say it. You don't know what happened to Johnson after you got away from them SP's. From that time until he got to the hospital, you don't know what happened. So, listen to me, Mart. I know. I wound up in the brig trying to be a nice guy. I wound up being accused falsely and I had a hell of a time getting it all squared away. Just don't say a word to nobody. Just forget it. Do you hear what I'm saying, do'ya know what I'm saying?"

"Yes," Martin answered weakly. He wanted to take this advice from his trusted friend. But his heart was heavy and his mind perplexed. "Yes, Scotty, I know what you are saying."

But he wasn't sure he could do what Scotty was recommending. He climbed into his bunk early that night and covered his head with his blanket to escape consciousness, to block out reality. He drifted into a reverie in which the words, "Jim Johnson is dead," resounded again and again. Then as sleep crept in, the reverie merged into a nightmare in which hundreds of shore patrolmen, all with the face of Johnson, chased him through the streets of Norfolk and from which he awoke sweating profusely and out of breath.

In the middle of the night, in darkness, he lay there wondering why he had ever joined the Navy. Maybe he should have continued his studies and then gone on to the seminary and married Alice Schneider. His thoughts focused on Alice and how she had responded when he told her about his plans that day back in April. My God, that was only five months ago. News broadcasts on the radio, and the newspapers, for weeks, had been detailing Germany's war and conquests in Europe. Debates in the U. S. Congress about the possibility of the U. S. getting into the war, and about the military draft, how 21 year-olds were being drafted into the Army, all this had left him unsettled. Graduation was approaching and he had to make some decisions. He had just stretched out on the campus lawn for a few minutes of quiet reflection, to think about what effect this would have on his life.

But this reflection had been interrupted when Alice walked up to him, and looking down affectionately, said, "Hey, Martin Miller, don't you know you'll catch something lying on the ground like that? This is Gettysburg, Pennsylvania, not Miami, Florida."

"Oh, don't worry, Allie," he'd said. "I'm in good shape." There was little meaning to his words. For, seeing her standing there from that angle, her graceful form showing faintly through her snugly fitting dress, brought perplexing thoughts to his mind. Desire, emanating from the area of his groin, surged through him and his whole body ached for want of her. Alice was about medium height, average, but slender. Her soft auburn hair, long and straight, hung almost to her waist. Her eyes were the darkest blue he had ever seen. In fact, they were more than blue, mixed perhaps with brown, some strange mixture of genes, different, but to Martin, alluring. He strained fervently to keep his hands and arms from reaching up and pulling her down to him. Those thoughts, to him, were disturbing thoughts of animal desire and lust which he couldn't suppress or shake off whenever she was near him.

"Hey, wake up, will you!" Alice shouted, annoyed by his apparent distraction.

"I'm sorry, Allie," he said, as he sat up, "I was just thinking."

"About what?" she asked, as she sat down alongside of him.

"Oh, about a lot of things, but mostly . . . I've been thinking about joining the Navy after graduation in May." He welcomed this opportunity to broach the subject.

"Join the Navy! Are you crazy?" Alice shouted as she jumped to her feet again.

"Now don't get excited," said Martin. "You've been reading the papers. Because of all this trouble in Europe the Navy is calling for men. They say if you serve one year on active duty in the Naval Reserve you won't be drafted into the Army. They are drafting men, you know."

"Yes, I know. But you would be exempt from the draft. I read only yesterday that anyone who is studying for the ministry, and some others, like pre-med students, won't be drafted."

"That's not the point, Allie. In the first place, I'm not so much in favor of being exempt from the draft, and besides, my Dad may be right. He says that a man should live and know something about life and people before he tries to be a minister to the people."

"But you're learning that here, aren't you? And you'll be going to the seminary too, you know," Alice said excitedly.

"Well, of course, I'm learning the history of religion and of Christianity. I'll be learning all about the dogma, and the ceremony of my church and when I'm through the seminary, I'll probably be well prepared to conduct church services and all of that. But, Alice, what experience will I have had with living, with life? With all of the courses I've had, and have yet to take, I think there will still be something missing."

"And you think a year in the Navy will help you find what's missing?" asked Alice, thoroughly perplexed.

"That's what I was thinking," he told her. But that wasn't all he was thinking. He didn't tell her that of late he was becoming increasingly disappointed with the method his professors were using to teach religion. He was confused by the fact that they were teaching religion the same way they taught the history of England, objectively, aloof, and untouched by its vast emotional appeal. He was impatient with their feigned scientific approach that was but a thin veil over a holier-than-thou attitude that held the organized church up as the final moral authority, but with tenets so stringent that its acceptance is impossible by the masses of people who are most in need of its moral guidance. He was also increasingly at odds with their insistence on belief in biblical events which were totally irrelevant to Christ's own teachings. But also Martin was aware that his own desire to become a minister in the Lutheran church was extremely vague and was becoming more clouded by the day. Was it because his grandfather, his mother's father, had been a Lutheran minister and she had often expressed how proud she would be if he were to follow in his grandfather's footsteps? At that moment he was at a complete loss to explain to anyone why he had chosen the ministry, and he knew he needed a change in his life, and time to sort it all out.

Alice again sat down alongside of him, and looked at him with her beautiful, understanding eyes. She waited for him to say more, but she sensed that his thoughts had drifted away from her.

"Your giving up the seminary to join the Navy sounds ridiculous to me," she said finally. "But I think I am the only one who understands you. Why don't you tell me what you are really thinking?"

"Well, part of it is this, Allie. I remember what my father said when I told him I was going into the ministry. He said, 'What the hell's gotten into you? You've been listening to your mother too much. Why, look here, son, I own one of the best damn little chemical plants in Pennsylvania. We make gun powder here that's in demand all over the world. I have a golden opportunity waiting for you here in the business, and by Jesus, I don't understand your wanting to do this. Can you explain this to me so it makes some sense?' But, you know, Alice, I couldn't explain it to him. I wonder if anyone ever makes the decision to become a minister or a priest on some rational basis. For me it was just a 'feeling' that that's what I should do, something like intuition. But now I have the 'feeling' that maybe it was a mistake. Do you know what I mean?"

"I don't know exactly, Martin, but I think maybe I'm getting the general idea," Alice said as she snuggled closer and transmitted to Martin that tenderness which can only be transmitted by a young girl in love. He put his arm around her and held her tightly, wanting to say so many things to her, but unable to find the words. No, he was not able to explain it to her either, because what he wanted to express was that vague desire which stems from a deep and fathomless inner soul and cries out within the breasts of some individuals, and commands them to seek out truth and then transmit it to their fellow human beings. Martin knew that he could have no rest or peace of mind unless he did this. But how? Was the ministry the right way to go? He was no longer sure that this was his calling.

Martin looked into the warmth of Alice's eyes. He ran his fingers through her soft auburn hair. He leaned over and rubbed her nose with his own. He looked at her moist, tempting lips. He kissed her. He felt her full response. Desire surged through him again. Suddenly he jumped up, bringing her up with him.

"Damn! Let's go get a soda and get away from here before I embarrass the both of us," Martin said, flushing.

"O. K.," said Alice. She blushed slightly as she recomposed herself.

They walked in silence toward the student center.

FIVE

Sex, Religion, and Guilt

As he lay there on his bunk in the darkness of the ship's crew quarters, trying to sort out the events of the recent past, he was only vaguely aware of his surroundings. He shut out the present and concentrated on the past. It was Alice, without a doubt. It was Alice Schneider who had become so entangled in his life during the past four years that he had no memory of the recent past without her in it. But he remembered now the feeling of a sense of loss as he and Alice left Gettysburg after graduation. It was a feeling of walking down the path to an unknown destination from which there was to be no return. Alice was more confident than he was that her college education was right for her. He wasn't so sure about his. She was proud of her Bachelor of Arts Degree in Psychology. He wasn't too sure about his in Pre-Theology. But he was proud of her.

He remembered the disappointment he felt when his mother wrote that his father was too busy at the plant to go to his graduation, and she couldn't make the trip without him. But Alice's parents had invited him to ride with them as far as Harrisburg. They drove in silence while they took in the beauty of the surroundings, stopping occasionally to gaze out over the Pennsylvania landscape. As they continued, Alice snuggled closer and closer to Martin. He became aware of her again sensually, and drew her tightly into his arms. They kissed several times when they thought her parents were not looking. Although the Schneiders were not as strict as some parents, Martin knew they disapproved of any public display of courtship antics.

In Harrisburg, before they parted, Alice promised to visit Martin's home the second week of June. They dropped Martin at the bus terminal. Then she and her parents went on their way northward along the Susquehanna River toward their home in Middleburg.

As the bus sped along the open highway, Martin had become aware of the enormity of nature. It had provided the fertile soil of this area to which his Pennsylvania German ancestors had been drawn during the colonial days. After years of toil there were now acres and acres of well kept farm lands, stately barns, and neat, white farm houses speckled across the land. And when he approached his home near Deitschtown, he filled with excitement as he always did after a long stay away. The big stone house, in the rural area west of town, which his paternal grandfather had built, looked solid and permanent, as if it would last forever. Generations of the descendents of German miners, farmers, quarrymen, explosives experts and stonemasons had preceded his father, and the house he lived in and the business which occupied his life reflected this heritage. Martin started up the front steps, a grip in each hand, then changed his mind and went through a side gate to the back of the house. He went quietly up the rear porch steps, put down the grips and knocked loudly on the screen door. There was a momentary silence, and then the click-click-click of familiar foot steps.

"What is it?" he heard his mother ask before reaching the door. When she looked out, she screamed, "Martin, Oh, my boy, why do you always surprise me like this?"

By this time she had the screen door open and was hugging him like she used to hug him when he was a little boy.

"You wrote us that you would come in on the 10 o'clock train Saturday morning."

"You know me, Mom. The Schneiders offered me a ride as far as Harrisburg, so naturally, I accepted."

"Naturally," said his mother. "I know you wouldn't miss any chance to be with that Alice. But, how are you?"

"Good as can be, Mom. I got all A's and B's in my courses.

"Oh, that's wonderful, Martin. Your brother Fred is a good boy, a steady worker, but you have ways of making me so proud."

"O. K., cut it out Mom, you'll give me a swell head. What've you got to eat?"

"We're having late supper tonight because your father phoned that he'd be coming home late from the plant. But he'll be here soon now."

Immediately after supper Martin had approached his father about his intentions of joining the Navy.

"Join the Navy! Good God, boy, don't let your mother hear you say that. Where the hell do you get such outlandish ideas? First you wanted to study for the ministry. Now you have spent four years doing that, and now you suddenly decide you want to join the Navy. Martin, I want to tell you something. The best thing in life is to have a job or a business so you can provide for and raise a family. Why don't you get these silly notions out of your head and take a job at the plant? Work hard and make something of yourself. Look at your brother Fred. He's been at the plant working hard for five years. I pay him a good salary. And if I died tonight, he could take over in my place. What could you do--pray?"

"Dad, you know what's going on. I'm sure you read the newspaper this morning. If I weren't going to college, I'd be drafted soon anyhow. Besides you're the one who said I should get some experience and learn about life."

"Well," his father replied, "you can learn about life right here in this town. How do you think Fred got his draft deferral? You know about some of the stuff we make at the plant. We've got orders for ammunition from England running out of our ears right now. And as far as Roosevelt getting us into the war, that's all talk, propaganda. They've been talking like that ever since World War I."

"Well, I'd like to join and serve on active duty for one year, anyhow. Will you back me up when I tell Mom?"

At that moment his mother entered the room and having heard the last part of the conversation, asked, "What are you two up to now? What must you tell me?"

They were both speechless for a moment.

"Your youngest son is going to join the Navy," his father said finally, very calmly.

"Join the Navy!" cried his mother, almost hysterically. "Martin, what do you mean? You can't be serious."

"Sure he's serious," his father answered, always reluctant to take his wife's side in any argument. "What's wrong with serving your country? Besides, it'll be a good experience for him to serve aboard ship as a seaman. He only wants to go for a year." He had talked himself into supporting Martin's position, perhaps out of pride or a secret wish that he had done that himself in the last war. "And as an ordinary sailor, not even as a Navy officer. Oh, you fools! This is ridiculous, it's terrible. Martin you know you only have . . ."

"Yes, yes, I know, Mom," he interrupted. "I have thought about it for a long time and I really want to go. For a year at least. After that I can go to the seminary. Let's not fight about it."

"Oh, what's the use. I can never get anywhere when you two stick together. I was so happy when you decided to become a minister, now you want to ruin it all. I'm going to bed," she said and stormed out of the room.

"She's very upset, Dad What do you . . .?"

"Let her alone, Mart. She'll get over it," his father had said.

He had wasted no time contacting the Navy Recruiting Office in the post office building. He took his physical exams, and then after acceptance, received his orders to report to the Navy Recruiting Office in Philadelphia. It all went so fast he barely remembered the details, but as soon as he had the dates set, he called Alice and urged her to visit him at his home as soon as possible.

He recalled vividly those days spent with Alice. They would be a part of his memory forever. On the day she arrived he browsed through various newspapers and magazines at the Lehigh Valley Railroad Station while he waited for the train. One of the magazines containing a story of the menacing German U-boats caught his eye. He bought the magazine and sat down on one of the long wooden benches in the waiting room. One of the stories in the magazine was an account of the British sinking of the

German battleship, the dreadnought "Bismarck," an exciting tale of the Royal Navy's superior strategy in destroying this symbol of Germany's invincibility. The story inflamed his imagination and confirmed for him that joining the Navy had been the right thing to do.

When he heard the screeching and hissing of the arriving train he quickly made his way out on the platform and searched for Alice in the rushing crowd. Finally he spotted her, a coat in one hand and a grip in the other. He rushed over to her and greeted her with such enthusiasm that she blushed with embarrassment.

"I'm sure glad to see you, Allie," he said. "I was so used to the two of bus being together so much of the time I just didn't realize I would miss you in a couple of weeks. I really missed you."

"I knew I would miss you, so I was glad when you called to ask me to come as soon as possible. Now what's the surprise?"

Martin didn't answer until they got into the car, but he could barely wait to tell her, "Well, I've joined the Navy."

"Oh, so you really did it?"

"Yes, and I'm leaving this coming Sunday."

"Then I won't be with you a full week."

"That's why I wanted you to come now."

"I knew you were thinking seriously about this, but I really didn't think you would go through with it. Now that you have gone and done it, I really don't know what to say." Tears filled her eyes. "This does affect all of our plans, Martin. I really thought you'd wait until after you had finished seminary."

"I know. Thinking about how this would affect us, was my biggest problem."

"Then why did you do it?"

"I'm not sure. It was all the things we discussed, and more. I guess I just had to do it."

Alice sniffled and took out a handkerchief. When they pulled up in front of the house, she powdered her nose and straightened her hair.

Martin's mother greeted Alice warmly and with great affection. He could tell by the look in his sister's eyes, that Margaret approved of Alice. He'd been right about that, Alice and Margaret got along really well, and he guessed a new, genuine friendship had been launched.

At dinner, apparently anxious to have everyone know, Alice announced: "I am going to the university in Chicago this fall for my Masters in Psychology."

"When did you decide that?"

"My professor in Child Psychology has been talking to me about it. He is moving up there to teach, and he thinks I should make a career of psychology. He says the field is wide open and there aren't enough women in it. I wasn't sure what to do, but now with Martin going into the Navy, I've decided to do it," she answered as she avoided Martin's questioning eyes.

"I was wondering what you thought of Martin running out on all of us like this," his mother said, looking at Alice.

"I'm not sure what to think. He does have a mind of his own, and when he decides he wants to do something, it's hard to change it."

"How well I know!" his mother said. "He's just like his father in that respect."

Martin and his father looked at each other, smiling sheepishly. But neither of them said anything.

When dinner was over, Martin was anxious to go somewhere alone with Alice, so he borrowed the car and they went into town to a movie.

Afterwards, Martin headed for a secluded spot on a nearby mountain ridge, where he had often gone as a teenager when he wanted to be alone. Now he wanted to be with Alice in a place where they could be alone, undisturbed. He guided the car expertly with one hand as the road began to wind its way upward and around the small mountain just outside of town. When they reached the top, he turned off into a winding dirt road, and followed it for about two miles into the woods. There they came upon a small clearing from which there was a full view of the town below them. It was outlined in both stationary and moving lights.

"Look how small our town appears, and yet, how bright and alive it is," Martin said.

"It's a wonderful view," answered Alice.

When Martin parked the car and turned off the engine, they were delighted by the strange quietness which surrounded them. They inhaled the cool, fresh night air. Then they became aware of the little sounds of nature--the sound of crickets, the buzzing of insects, the crackling of leaves, stirred by the soft wind. The area was devoid of all man-made sound, and Martin became infected with that beauty of nature which does not have to be seen to be appreciated. It was the beauty of nature that he could feel; it was soothing, yet stimulating to his whole being.

He leaned back into the corner on his side of the car, stretching his long legs out towards the other side. He drew Alice into his arms, and she willingly snuggled her head onto his chest. For a long time they remained in this position, still and silent, taking in the beauty of the night, glad to be together, alone. They began to pet, pressing the sides of their faces together, prolonging breathless kisses, talking of bygone days, and of future days, feeling glad to be together, alone.

But slowly, uncontrollably, those thoughts came back to Martin again to mar for him the beauty of the moment. They were thoughts which caused him great conflict; they were feelings, urges, in which he envisioned himself chasing Alice the way he had seen spirited horses on nearby farms go after their mates. But his conscious mind lashed out and fought vehemently against these instinctive inclinations.

Alice beside him, so warm, so tender, her breath falling warm upon his neck, could not have realized she wasn't helping him in his struggle against the animal desire that was raging within him.

Finally, Martin took Alice firmly by the shoulders and shoved her gently away from him.

"We'll have to stop this. I can't handle this. I love you too much. I respect you too much. This will lead to no good."

"I'm not sure what you mean."

"Oh, Alice, you know what I mean. Look . . . for the past three years or more . . . all the time we spent together . . . we love each other . . . but we've denied each other. But I know we should be married to do what I'm thinking."

"Oh, of course, I know what you mean. I know it's confusing. But we can't go all the way. My parents would kill me if they ever found out that I would go all the way. We just can't."

"Yeah, and according to the church it would be . . . it'd be fornication. It'd be a sin."

"Well, I think that's debatable. One of my psychology professors said, or at least implied, that it's not wrong if you don't get pregnant. But I know there's more to it than that. Still I find the idea of it being a sin hard to accept."

"Yeah, it is one of the things I also find hard to accept. But Jesus himself said that . . . "

"Oh, for Heaven's sake, Martin," cried Alice, angry and ashamed for having admitted what she was thinking. Let's forget about religion and psychology and all that. Let's just be ourselves."

"Oh, Alice," Martin moaned. "If only we could really be ourselves and do what we really want to do and not regret it. It's all so damned confusing. Why do I desire you so much? Why do I want to make you a part of my own body? Why do I have these deep, urgent feelings of desire and need and love for you, and then feel guilty about these feelings? What is this all about anyway? There must be some answer to this problem. It's not only sex. The feelings are more than that."

"What?" Alice whispered.

"They're feelings of want, of needing, not of lust, but of a deeper need, an indescribable hunger, emanating from deep inside of me--something manifesting or trying to become or . . . Oh dammit, Alice, I can't wait any longer."

He eased her down on the full length of the car seat, and gently massaged her. They both began to perspire, and to breathe rapidly.

"Martin, this is making me very nervous," Alice said. "I'm sorry, but I'm, I'm scared. We can't go all the way. Oh, what's the matter with us. We're not children anymore. But you better stop right now, or . . ." She began to shake nervously all over, but, almost instinctively, reached down and grabbed hold of him.

He entered her like a raging, overly aroused bull. But the fury lasted only a few short minutes. Then it was over, it was done, and an overwhelming remorse, like a heavy cloud settled in upon them.

"Oh, Martin, what a mess you've made," said Alice, angry and disillusioned. "I thought there would be more to it than that."

He helped her sit up again and held her tightly as tears began to stream down both of their faces. Remorse permeated the atmosphere and mingled with the odors of earthiness and human perspiration.

Martin began to feel again the sense of loss, the sense of the end of an era, the end of school days and romantic love, and the feeling of the present merging dialectically into a new life of undreamed of reality. They drove down the mountain in silence.

The next day they went shopping together and picked out a diamond engagement ring. They announced their engagement that evening at dinner. No one had seemed surprised.

SIX

Indoctrination

It was like a raging whirlwind that had swept him up with everything else in its path. It twisted and twirled and mangled and reshaped his life and then dropped him in a strange new place. But it was also as if he himself had caused the whirlwind. He could not blame it on circumstances, or on God, for he knew it had been his own decision which brought about these events of the recent past.

He twisted and turned upon his bunk as he lay there in the darkness of the crew's quarters remembering those whirlwind days. Alice had pleaded with him to change his mind about joining the Navy. He left her in tears at the railroad station the day he left for Philadelphia to report to the district recruiting station. Then, with the words from the "Oath of Allegiance" still ringing in his ears, "I, Martin Miller, do solemnly swear that I will bear true faith and allegiance to the United States of America, and that I will serve them honestly and faithfully against all their enemies whomsoever, and that I will obey the orders of the President of the United States and orders of the officers appointed over me, according to the rules and articles for the government of the Navy," several days later, he had found himself at the United States Naval Training Station, Newport, Rhode Island.

The following weeks of indoctrination into the military service, he decided, were probably more important than he anticipated. For there followed one thing after another for which he had been totally unprepared. This period was to bridge the gap between civilian life and the coming military life. It was the period when the individual man had to learn to submerge his individuality, to surrender himself and become an integral part of the group personality. And the change-over was accomplished primarily by doing everything as a group.

But submerging the individuality was not easy, as he learned one day when one of the other recruits in his company kicked him in the rear end and shouted, "Get the hell out of my way, you freakin' landlubber." He had been tired from the incessant drilling. His anger rose quickly whenever he was extremely tired. He turned around and grabbed this man by the neck. It was Scott Ackermun, a man with whom Martin had had words several times before. He was several years older than Martin, of medium build, stocky and muscular. He was uncouth and vulgar, and his speech was speckled with those telltale and distinctive characteristics that branded him as "Pennsylvania Dutch," a descendant of the Pennsylvania Germans who originated from Martin's own area, one of his own ethnic group.

The two of them squared off immediately, but were promptly stopped by the company commander. "Any fighting by Navy men has to be an organized grudge fight. You fight according to the rules and under supervision," the CO told them.

Martin had welcomed the match, and in a refereed bout of six, two minute rounds, he knew his opponent was a good match. It was good to have the gloves on again. He had been in constant training as a member of the college boxing team for the past two years and he was in excellent physical condition. He had natural energy and vitality and by the end of the fifth round he knew he had Scott Ackermun beaten, but Scott would not give up.

The CO congratulated Martin after the fight. "You've got good form, kid, and powerful hands. You should look into joining one of the official Navy boxing teams when you get through 'boot camp.' And watch out you don't hurt somebody".

After the fight he and Scotty became friends. He had beaten Scotty because Scotty was not a trained fighter. Had it been a street fight, it may have ended differently, for Scotty was tough and Martin respected his toughness as well as his ability and his good sportsmanship. He wasn't quite sure, at first, why Scotty wanted to become his friend. On the surface it appeared they didn't have much in common, except that they were from the same ethnic background.

Scotty was born on a farm near Kutztown, Pennsylvania, but grew up and attended public school in Bethlehem. Because of the depression of the 1930's, his father had to give up the farm and take a job with the Bethlehem Steel Company. Scotty quit school after he completed ninth grade, got working papers and went to work as a plumber's apprentice for a local plumbing shop. After several years of that, he had joined the Navy. He had served the four years of a regular enlistment. But he didn't like Navy life well enough to make it a career, he told Martin, and therefore did not re-enlist at the end of his first hitch. Then, with rumors of war and the draft call, he had re-enlisted. As with all men who had previous service, but not continuous service, he was required to go through 'boot camp' again.

Martin vividly remembered the night he was sitting on the wooden steps of the barracks in a dejected mood. Scotty had walked up to him and said, "What's eatin' ya, Parson?"

"Oh, I don't know," he had answered. "This life isn't exactly what I thought it would be."

"Aw, don't worry about it," Scotty had said, in his husky voice. "This ain't the real Navy. You won't have to put up with this kind of crap if you get duty on a good ship. Besides this boot training will be over in a couple of weeks. I went through it before, you know, and it was the same old shit then as it is now."

"Well, I guess it's really not that bad. I'm probably just getting impatient. I guess I was expecting to see ships right away, not barracks and drill fields. By the way, what made you call me 'Parson'?"

"I didn't mean nothin' by it," said Scotty. "I heard you was a-studyin' to be a preacher before you signed up. I know one of the Yeoman in the personnel office. Me and him served together when I did my first hitch. He told me."

"Are you interested in religion?"

"Naw, not really. But I often wondered about some of the things we learned when I was a kid. They made me go to Sunday school. There was a lotta things there I couldn't understand."

"What church do your parents go to?"

"They're Lutherans. My father was German Reformed, and my mother was Lutheran, but we went to a union church. That's where they met. It had both Lutheran and Reformed Congregations. When they got married my father changed."

"My parents were both born Lutherans," Martin said.

"My parents got divorced after we moved into town," Scotty interrupted. "My mother said seven kids was enough, she didn't want no more, and my old man, he didn't make enough money to feed us all as it was. After that they didn't go to church much, especially the old man. But they used to make us go to Sunday school at the Lutheran church. That's where I first learned about cunts, girls, I mean. I got one of them in the broom closet and she let me play with everything she had. Then I had just talked her into making believe we was grown-ups in bed when the janitor opened the door and, boy, did we get hell for that! I thought sure they would send me to reformed school after the girl said it was all my idea. But the Sunday school didn't want no publicity about it and they all made some kind of deal to hush it up."

As crude and vulgar as Scotty was, there was something basically good, though indefinable, about him that Martin liked. After that night they were constant companions. Scotty was always eager to tell, and Martin anxious to hear, stories of Navy life as Scotty had experienced it. They were an odd pair; Scotty with little formal education, but always self-assured and confident; and Martin, a college graduate, but without experience, always hesitant and unsure of this way in life.

Martin remembered the night he was in the recreation room making his daily entries in a letter to Alice. Scotty came over and stood in front of him for several minutes without speaking. Then finally he said: "You must really have a big crush on that gal, the way you keep on writin' her every day."

"Yes, we're engaged and we promised to write each other every day, even if it is just a few words. So I write something every day and then mail it about once a week. Don't you have a girlfriend back home?"

"Naw, not anymore, I don't. I used to have one, but we broke up just before I signed up for my second hitch. She was O. K., I guess. She was a good-lookin' babe, and really good in bed. But she wanted to follow me around all the time. And she was always on my back about getting a haircut, taking a bath, or buying new clothing. She was always trying to make me into a different man. I guess she and I were really in love. We sure did hit it off in bed. But she was always pushing to get married. She wanted to cook for me, and wash and iron for me, and clean my rooms and all that stuff. She reminded me a lot of my mother. She sure was pretty. But we broke up. I guess I just wasn't ready for all that. But sometimes I really do miss her. Yeah, she was O. K., I guess."

Martin was about to continue writing when Scotty interrupted again. "I've been talking to that Yeoman in the office. He said he could fix it so our names would go on a list to be assigned to a battlewagon, when we get through with this 'boot camp.' I hear that's the best duty in the Navy. How about it, should I tell him to fix it for the two of us?"

Duty on a battleship! That had exciting possibilities. He thought it over carefully before answering. He was amazed, if not somewhat doubtful, that Scotty would be able to make such arrangements.

"I think that'd be great, really great. If we could get duty together on a battleship. That sounds interesting. Do you think your friend could really arrange that?"

"Sure," Scotty had said, confidently. "They don't have no special method for picking guys for duty. Not for deck hands anyhow. They just take so many names from a list and send them wherever Washington tells them they need seamen. It don't make no difference to them who goes."

"O. K., then let's do it," Martin had said enthusiastically, elated by the prospects of such illustrious duty, and by the fact that he was choosing the course of his own future. He had made his own decision and had looked forward to the future with anticipation and excitement.

But, Martin had soon learned, that there is perpetual conflict between man's idea of freedom, one's ability to choose the course of one's own future, and predestination or determinism, the idea that each event in nature and in people's lives is caused by a preceding event, and that each preceding event was determined by an event preceding it, ad infinitum, as he had read somewhere in a text book. He wondered if there was really some greater outside force at work deliberately manipulating the events? Or was it pure chance, or cruel fate that had caused his plans to be so radically altered. He was not sure. There must be something wrong with both of those theories, he thought.

They had had choices. They had chosen. But, certainly, the plans he and Scotty had made and looked forward to with such pleasure and excitement had surely gone awry! Their orders, so eagerly anticipated, had come through for assignment to general sea duty, with instructions to report to the U. S. Naval Receiving Station, Norfolk, Virginia, after a one week boot leave. They assumed this was in response to the request they had made through Scotty's Yeoman friend in the office.

They took the train together to Pennsylvania. Scotty got off at Bethlehem and Martin continued on to Deitschtown. Alice had returned to Chicago to start the fall term at the university and he would not be able to see her. A visit to his father's plant left him bored, as it always did, and since there was no one close to him interested in his new venture, he just loafed for several days, and then contacted Scotty and made plans to leave for Norfolk, Virginia, a day early.

On the second day at the Receiving Station where they were awaiting their expected assignment to a battleship, their names were called over the station loudspeakers. Scotty was in the recreation room shooting pool and Martin had gone to the library. There was no loudspeaker in the library and Martin did not know that his name was being called. Hours later, Scotty rushed into the library and motioned for Martin to come outside.

"Hurry up," he said excitedly. "The Chief Boatswain at the Transfer Office is ravin' mad. He's been calling your name on one of the P. A. systems for several hours. Our orders are in. We're supposed to pack our bags and be ready to leave in the next hour."

"Why didn't you come up to the library and tell me?"

"I couldn't remember where the hell you went, but I shoulda guessed."

As he stepped up to the Chief's desk, he stood at attention and said, "I'm Martin Miller."

"Miller," said the Chief, glaring at him. "Where the goddamn hell have you been?"

"At the library, Sir. All afternoon."

"At the library," the Chief roared. "Well, that's a hell of a goddamn place for a sailor."

Martin turned red with anger and indignation at the abusive language.

"Here's your orders," said the Chief. "Your ship's in and you are due at the pier in twenty minutes. Now shake a leg."

Back at the barracks they read their orders in disbelief.

"A fleet tug--what the hell!" Scotty said. "I'll get that fat-assed yeoman for this."

"I thought you said we were getting duty on a battle-ship," said Martin. "What's a fleet tug?"

"It's a big, seagoing tug, that's what it is. It's big for a tug, but it's one of the smallest seagoing ships in the fleet. Although, the new ones are almost as big as a destroyer."

Later, as they stood on the pier watching their ship coming in to tie up, Martin felt a strange, new excitement welling up within him. The ship moved slowly, steadily toward the pier. Martin was speechless. As it drew near, he could hear the sound of the engines being reversed, and hear the rushing of the water as it was suddenly churned in the opposite direction. His excitement was intense. His heart pounded furiously.

"That's a beauty," Scotty had said as he observed the vessel on which all was "spit and polish."

But in Martin's mixed emotions he knew that he was almost scared of it. It was like a strange creature, grotesque and powerful. Although a fleet tug may be con-sidered a small ship by the Navy, and a "beauty" by Scotty, to Martin, it looked huge and ugly. Not only was this the first time Martin had come so close to ships, but it was to be the first time he had ever been aboard one.

As the ship's side screeched and scrapped along the pier, seaman in neatly pressed, white suits could be seen lined up along the rail; and others in blue dungarees heaved lines over the side to the dock. The engines made one last loud roar, then stopped. For a brief moment there was silence and order all around; then various strange noises and voices were heard from the ship. A gang plank was lowered over the side. The shrill tone of a Boatswains's pipe could be heard, as an officer, striped with gold braid came down the gang plank, followed by other officers with less gold.

"That must be the Captain," said Martin, under his breath.

As the group of officers approached them he became quite tense. They both saluted when the officers came within the proper range. Following the officers, was the group of sailors in neatly pressed, white uniforms. Each man saluted the officer at the top of the gang plank, who, Martin learned, was called the Officer-of-the-Deck, and each also saluted the flag on the fantail of the ship as he went over the side and down the gang plank. The liberty party hurried away.

"Holy Jesus," Scotty said. "I ain't never seen or heard of a fleet tug bein' that regulation. The skipper is probably real chickenshit. Well, let's get aboard." He grabbed his sea bag and slung it over his shoulder. Martin followed suit, and was glad that he was with his reassuring friend as they climbed aboard.

He forgot all about saluting the colors and the Officer-of-the-Deck, and he forgot the words which he had rehearsed over and over, "I am reporting aboard for duty, Sir," which he had been taught was the proper thing to say.

The Officer-of-the-Deck was formal, but not as abrupt as Martin had expected. He welcomed them aboard, but without wasting words, he told them to report to the ship's office for assignment to their berths.

"A couple of boots coming aboard," someone yelled as they were being led below decks by the O.D.'s messenger. In the office they handed their orders to the ship's yeoman.

"A couple of seamen," he said. "Well, we sure need seamen. The Boatswain's Mate has been yapping about being short-handed on the deck force." He wrote something on a slip of paper and handed it to the messenger. "Take them aft, Porter," he said, jokingly, but rather sarcastically, "and show them to their rooms."

They followed the messenger through various hatchways and compartments, through the mess hall, where the evening meal was being served, down to a lower deck into the crew's quarters. They were assigned bunks and lockers, Scotty on the one side of the compartment and Martin on the other.

"Hey, Johnson," yelled the messenger. "Here's a couple of new men for the deck gang. Take them in tow. I've got to get back up to the O. D."

The man whom he had addressed, Martin could see, was about his own height, but probably heavier. He was a First Class Boatswain's Mate. As he came up to them, Martin was on the verge of extending his hand to introduce himself, when the Boatswain said rudely, "I'm Jim Johnson, boatswain in charge of the deck gang. You'll be working for me. You're just in time for chow. After chow you can get your gear squared away. Then you'll be off until the morning, but you can't go ashore. In the morning you fall out with the deck gang at quarters."

In the mess hall the odor of the food was strong and metallic. The air was hot and stuffy. Martin was too excited to eat, but he took the ice cream and coffee.

Later they went out on the main deck and examined the ship. Some men nodded as they passed, recognizing them as newcomers, but others ignored them. The sun was just beginning to sink below the horizon as they walked up forward to the point of the bow, the highest point on the main deck. They looked out over the bay to the other ships. Then they walked down the other side. Here and there men were reading, straining their eyes under the dim rays of the failing sun. Up on the bridge, the area from which the ship is navigated, they could see several men who, although on duty, were doing nothing, just waiting for time to pass.

Then, they went back to the crew's quarters. The events of this first day, reporting for duty aboard his first ship, had been exhausting for Martin, and when he had climbed into his new bunk that night he immediately dropped off into dreamless sleep.

The next morning he was awakened with a start. There was a sharp ringing crack on the bottom of his bunk, which was produced by the swift swinging of a night stick by Boatswain's Mate First Class, Jim Johnson, as he went through the rows of bunks rousing the crew, arrogantly shouting: "Rise and shine, Sailors, rise and shine. Rise and shine, Sailors, we have work to do."

And every morning had been the same thereafter, for several weeks, aboard the USS FLEET TUG.

SEVEN

Liberty in New York City

Martin knew that he had cut himself off from home and family and school and career. He knew that his actions had forced Alice to go down a new path which resulted in her deserting him, and now he felt the utter void of being adrift without the roots and ties that had previously provided his security. He was alone like a piece of driftwood, floating and tossed about in the vastness of the open sea. He would now have to look elsewhere for solace and security.

With these thoughts he had finally drifted off into a troubled sleep. But now he was awakening again, awakening into the world of the present, for no matter where our thoughts may take us, Martin realized, we cannot for long ignore the reality in which we actually exist. He was hearing the same sharp ringing crack again at the bottom of his bunk. He was hearing again the same rousing words, "Rise and shine, Sailors. Rise and shine. Rise and shine, Sailors, we have work to do." But this time it was not Jim Johnson's voice calling out the "Rise and shine!" No, Jim Johnson was dead!

Was he, Martin Miller, responsible? Would he have to forever carry the burden of this guilt on his shoulders? He turned over and buried his face in his pillow, thinking that at a time like this he should try prayer.

"God damn it, Miller," the Chief Boatswain's Mate shouted. "Get the hell out of that sack!"

Martin jumped out and dressed quickly.

The Chief spieled off the following: "Uniform of the day for all hands is dungarees and rain gear. Repeat, uniform of the day is dungarees and rain gear. We will prepare to cast off at 0930. We will prepare to cast off at 0930. All hands muster on the fantail at 0900. All hands muster on the fantail at 0900."

There was a heavy overcast and drizzle as the ship's engines started with a roar, sending vibrations throughout the ship. But the Captain had planned a speech and he was not about to let a little drizzle stop him. All men and officers stood at attention on the fantail, on the main deck, wearing their black rain gear. It was a somber sight.

The Captain stepped out on the quarter deck overlooking the fantail. He spoke in a booming voice without the help of a loudspeaker.

"Men, for those of you who don't know, I am Commander Harry B. Mills, the Captain of your ship. I have just been informed that we have been reassigned to the Pacific Fleet, but we have a couple of jobs to do here on the East Coast before we head west.

"This is an auxiliary ship. It is a work ship. It is a mercy ship. But it is also an American Naval fighting ship, and before long we will be sailing with the fleet. We work for other Navy ships--give them emergency power, pull them off the beach if they ago aground, fight shipboard fires, tow them, but we can also use our antiaircraft guns and depth charges when necessary--anything that will help keep the Navy's fighting ships afloat, safely. That's our mission."

"The ship's complement of officers and men on this ship has been increased and almost half of the ship's crew have just come aboard within the past few days. But we have experienced, old hands in charge of all divisions, below in the engine room, as well as topside on deck and on the bridge. We have a new executive officer, Lieutenant Frank Rosetto. He is up on the bridge right now plotting our course for our next port-of-call. You'll get to know him within the next few days, I'm sure. I want to remind all hands that following orders is the most important thing that will be required of you. I run a tight ship, because that's what makes a safe ship. On a fleet tug like we have here, we sometimes get some very hazardous assignments, and a tight run ship usually comes through. So remember to follow orders. Anyone who does not, will be dealt with severely."

"Our next port-of-call will be the Philadelphia Navy Yard. We'll be towing that old four-stacker destroyer that you see anchored out there in the bay off of our starboard bow. After that we'll be heading for the Brooklyn Navy Yard without a tow. We'll be up there for several days getting some repairs."

"I want to personally welcome all you new men aboard. It has often been said that duty aboard a seagoing fleet tug is 'good duty.' I hope you'll find it that way. Smooth sailing to you all. Now, all hands dismissed. Report to your stations and prepare to get underway."

The Captain was a lieutenant-commander by rank, Martin learned later. This was not his first command. He had previously commanded a submarine tender. But the tender had run aground due to a navigational miscalculation. It wasn't actually the Captain's fault. He had trusted his navigator. But as Navy tradition had it the captain had to take responsibility for the mistake. Actually he was lucky to get another command.

After the Captain's speech, the Chief Boatswain ordered the deck gang to remain. "Because of Jim Johnson's death, I'll be directly in charge of the deck gang myself. I'll repeat what the Captain said. Everything will go well if everybody obeys orders. Each of you has your assigned duty station, and you'll get your orders from me. Follow your orders and all will be well. On this cruise we'll have four hours on and eight hours off. This will give every man plenty of practice on his duty station and plenty of time for training sessions. If you have any questions, you see me."

"Prepare to get underway," the Executive Officer's voice came through the loudspeakers.

"Cast off all lines," he said later. And then, "Half speed ahead--Easy left rudder--Steady as you go."

They steamed out into the Chesapeake Bay, headed for the old four-stacker destroyer. When they pulled alongside, Scotty was instructed to throw them a line. Attached to this line was a heavier manila line and to that was attached the fleet tug's steel cable. This was pulled aboard the destroyer by use of a winch and attached to the destroyer's bow.

The USS FLEET TUG moved away slowly until the tow cable was taut, then more cable was let out until it formed a large arched cable between the two vessels.

Martin could hear the command, "Weigh anchor," from the other ship in response to signals from his own ship's bridge. Then they were underway, headed for the narrow channel at the mouth of the bay, with the four-stacker destroyer in tow.

As they steamed out of the Chesapeake Bay, and then northward, hugging the coast line, Martin decided to put all thoughts of Jim Johnson out of his mind, and likewise thoughts of Alice. He had had enough of introversion, of self-examination. He had come to the conclusion that there was nothing he could do under the circumstances to change either situation. He could not change the fact of Johnson's death, nor could he now, heading out to sea, do anything about Alice's decision to marry another man. He had no choice now but to shut these thoughts out of consciousness. He was powerless to do anything about them and there was no point to dwelling on the feelings of impotence and frustration which they engendered. In fact, it was easier now to put these thoughts out of mind because other matters demanded his immediate attention. But he had not been prepared by any previous experience for what ensued during the next several days.

Only a few hours out of Norfolk, rough weather blew up suddenly. A storm out over the Atlantic, the most drab and the cruelest of seas, travelling northward, unexpectedly veered in an inland direction and engulfed the small convoy of ships in which they were travelling. The noon chow had just been finished. Martin reported back to the deck gang to continue on a work detail, stowing lines and hawsers. Suddenly be became weak all over, and his knees no longer could hold his weight. He grabbed hold of the life line running along the ship's rail on the main deck. He stood still for a moment, then tried to move on. He shook his head but could not shake off the dizziness. Saliva began to flow freely in his mouth. He approached the other men of the work detail, looking white as a ghost. He expected to be ridiculed, but surprisingly was not. However, the Chief Boatswain's Mate, yelled, good-naturedly, "Come on, Sailors, let's turn to, we've got work to do."

With every ounce of effort Martin had, he tried to do the work assigned to him, but finally, he just let go. He was so sick and weak he lay on the deck, face down. One of the other seaman rushed over to the rail, leaned over and threw up. That did it. Martin followed him, and in that swift moment of violent vomiting and retching he wished he were dead. He was so weak he couldn't lift himself off the rail where he had draped himself. The ship was pitching and rolling dangerously, nearly throwing him overboard. The other seaman grabbed hold of him and let him down gently on the deck.

"Call the Pharmacist's Mate," he said weakly. But by the time the Pharmacist's Mate arrived, having rid himself of what was in his stomach, he regained his equilibrium and felt the strength coming back into his legs.

"I'll make it to the sickbay on my own," he said, angrily. The storm continued its savagery for two more days, and they made very little headway. At one point they had to let go of the tow line attached to the old four-stacker, reel it in, and later go through the process of taking it in tow again after the storm abated. Finally, they reached the Delaware Bay, which was a welcome relief, and they sailed smoothly up to the Philadelphia Navy Yard.

They stayed only long enough to deliver the destroyer to its assigned berth, and then headed out again and set their course for the port of New York. Throughout most of the trip Scotty had very little to say. Martin surmised that he too must have had trouble adjusting himself to the sea, getting his sea-legs, as old-timers called it, so he didn't question him about his silence. But, Martin noticed that there may have been something else bothering him which seemed to be causing him to avoid conversation.

In his position as Seaman, Second Class, Martin felt somewhat like an outsider and he knew that it would probably take a long time before he was accepted as one of the regulars. He also learned that, even on a ship as small as this, there existed a military "caste system," a ranking of individuals according to their present Navy rank or rating. Each rank had a clique of its own. Each succeeding higher rank held itself above and aloof from the next lower rank. He made several attempts to cross those caste system lines by being genuinely friendly and congenial, but it never worked very well. One of the officers told him frankly that he had been taught that "familiarity breeds contempt" and that officers were not to fraternize with enlisted men. The officers lived in another world of their own, and on this small ship that meant they spent most of their time on the bridge, in the officers' wardroom, or in their separate state-rooms. "Officer's country," as it was called, was a relatively small area.

The day of their arrival in New York, they tied up to a pier in the Brooklyn Navy Yard. Liberty was granted to two-thirds of the officers and men. Fortunately, Martin thought, he and Scotty were allowed to go with the first liberty party, which would have liberty until the following morning at 0900.

"What do you plan to do when we get into the city?" Scotty asked as they left the Navy Yard.

"My sister Margaret lives here in Manhattan. At least she has an apartment and stays here most of the time. She also goes home a lot on weekends. She works as a secretary for some big industrial company. I'm going to call her as soon as we get into the city. What are your plans?"

"Well, I gotta dig me up some nice ripe tomato. I'm overdue. I didn't make out at all in Norfolk."

"What do you mean a ripe tomato?"

"You know. A babe. New York is full of them. You can't miss here."

"I thought maybe you would want to go along with me to visit my sister. Why don't you forget about the 'babes' and come along?"

"Well, Mart, knowin' the kind of guy you are, and I don't mean to insult ya, I don't think I would want to be goin' to where your sister is, 'cause I'm sure she ain't no tomato. That wouldn't be no place for me, considerin' the condition I'm in."

"What do you mean?"

"Aw, you know what I mean."

"You mean you just want to find a girl for sexual intercourse? You mean you want a prostitute?"

"Well, no, not exactly a prostitute. I wasn't thinking of a prostitute. I just mean something that looks pretty good to have a few dances and a couple of drinks with, and then wind up having a good time in bed. You know, get my tubes cleaned out. I'm not planning to pay for it, not directly anyhow. Unless that's the last resort. Of course, you know what they say, 'any old port in a storm.' What the hell! You know that."

"That's a foul way to think about the relationship between a man and a woman. Sex is supposed to be a sincere relationship. It's for married people," Martin said sternly. Suddenly he thought of Alice and he cringed. "It's for people who love each other," he forced out. Then sadness gripped him.

"Aw, shoot," said Scotty. "Look, I don't mean to belittle you or nothin' like that. But I was brought up with that kind of idea too. Maybe you won't believe it, knowing me as you do, but I was. But after a few years on my own, I learned different. How do you think you would feel if you had to go to the toilet but you didn't go for days and days or weeks and weeks. You'd likely get pretty damn sick, wouldn't you? Well, it's the same with sex. Nature demands that you get rid of it every now and then. Your balls generate so much of that sperm, and then by God you gotta get rid of it. And there ain't nothin' like a good, old-fashioned jazzin' with a woman. Taking care of yourself is O. K. when there ain't no women around. But you gotta get rid of it somehow, and you can't sweat it out of your ribs. I know, I tried everything already, but there ain't nothin' like a good woman."

Martin turned red from his neck to his hair line upon hearing this line of reasoning. He choked up and spoke angrily. "Your morals are outrageous. Let's drop it."

"O. K., suits me. But you'll see what I mean some day, just wait."

Both were silent as they walked several blocks to the subway station. Martin thought of Alice again and felt the anger boiling inside again, and then he thought of Jim Johnson. The anger subsided, then remorse set in again and feelings of guilt overwhelmed him. He continued the silence. He was glad Scotty was with him. He needed a friend.

"I tell you what I'd like to do," Scotty said finally, recognizing Martin's gloom. "I'll go along up to your sister's place this afternoon. Then tonight I'll take off downtown."

Martin hesitated a moment, undecided after the conversation they had just had whether he should take Scotty along. "That's O. K. with me," he said, hesitantly, "but remember, my sister, Margaret, is no tomato."

As the taxi sped across the bridge to Manhattan, he wondered several times if it was a mistake to take Scotty along to meet Margaret. He had second thoughts about this, but it was too late now. What Martin really needed was time to talk with Margaret. She was a good listener, and she often came up with good suggestions. He also needed time to think, to plan, to decide what to do about Alice. Oh, God, what could he do about Alice? What little effort he had made had accomplished nothing. He hadn't even written to her as yet, nor had he talked to her. He seemed to have a mental block whenever he thought about her. Ordinarily he knew that he would have gotten the train and headed for Chicago immediately after receiving her letter. But these were not ordinary circumstances. He was in the Navy now, and he couldn't just get up and go whenever he felt like it.

Then, as the taxi came down off the bridge and wound its way through the city traffic, and as he took in the sights of New York, these thoughts were again crowded out of his consciousness. And fate, or whatever it is that brings about such circumstances, brought about a new event which threw him off his intended course and added a new entanglement to his already entangled life. His freedom, his volition, his freedom to choose, which he had exercised, was once again thwarted by antecedent causes of a devious nature. He met Angela Rosetto!

EIGHT

A Small World

When they arrived at Margaret's apartment, she had just returned from work. It was Saturday and she worked only until noon.

"Well, this is certainly a surprise!" she exclaimed as she unlocked the door. "I never expected to see you so soon. I thought you would be somewhere on the high seas by this time."

"It's good to see you too," Martin said, smiling broadly and pinching her cheek as he always did when greeting her. "But, let me tell you this; we just came from the highest seas I ever want to see. The Atlantic Ocean in a storm was my initiation into the realm of the high seas. Right, Scotty?"

"Right," answered Scotty eying Margaret from her head to her toes and back again.

"Margaret, I want you to meet Scott Ackermun. Scotty, this is my sister, Margaret."

"I'm pleased to meet ya," Scotty said, showing intense interest. "Martin has been sayin' nice things about ya."

"I'm pleased to meet you," she answered. "I remember Martin mentioning your name. Weren't you the one he had the fight with up at Newport, Rhode Island?"

"You remembered right. Martin beat the stuffin's outa me, that's how we got to be friends."

"Yeah, then we got fouled up together. Would you believe it, we're on a seagoing tug, a fleet tug, and now we're in the Brooklyn Navy Yard for some repairs."

The apartment had a large living room, one bedroom, a bath and a small kitchen. Margaret was aglow with excitement as she scurried about picking up things and getting lunch together. Their conversation was rapid as they brought each other up to date on the events of the past several months. Martin painfully and deliberately related the contents of Alice's letter, as if, by bringing this painfulness to the surface he was trying to heal himself from its painful effects. He also wanted to tell her about Jim Johnson, but his mind was now rejecting the memory of it, and he avoided the subject.

Scotty didn't have much to say, as was often his way, but he didn't miss a thing. He couldn't keep his eyes off of Margaret. He followed her every movement as she darted back and forth from the stove to the refrigerator and from the kitchen to the little dining alcove off the kitchen. Her graceful movements gave tiny rippling waves to the clothing covering her buttocks and breasts. When Martin caught him starring at her, Scotty flushed with embarrassment, a rare thing for him.

Gradually, however, Margaret drew him into the conversation, and while they all ate lunch together, a warm and homey atmosphere pervaded the apartment.

"I know that you two don't want to waste your liberty sitting around here," Margaret said. "What would you like to do this afternoon?"

"Oh, I just wanted to visit with you. But Scotty had something else in mind," Martin answered.

"Nothin' really definite," Scotty injected quickly.

"Well," said Margaret, "I don't have anything special planned either. A girlfriend of mine, Angela Rosetto, and I were going to do a little shopping this afternoon. That's all. It sure is a good thing this is not one of the weekends I go home. I would have missed seeing you. Would you like to see a show? I can usually get tickets for the matinee of almost any of the shows."

"Sounds good to me," said Martin.

"Same here," said Scotty, looking as if he were going to reach out and grab Margaret any instant.

"You wouldn't mind if Angela comes along, would you? She is due here any minute."

They all agreed, so Margaret made several phone calls to arrange for the tickets.

Martin didn't know why, but when Angela arrived and they were being introduced, he became unusually excited. He hadn't pictured her anything at all like she actually was. She was of medium height, slender, with long dark hair, dark eyes and had the appearance of one of those girls whose pictures he had often seen in the society pages of the newspaper. She was full of that vitality and nervous energy which is displayed by the slick race horses when they are restrained at the starting gate. She had an accent, however, which didn't seem to go with her appearance. It marked her as a native New Yorker. She was a definite contrast to Margaret, who was tall, had blonde hair and blue eyes, and who spoke in that flat, nondescript accent which she had developed during her college days.

Margaret reminded them that if they wanted to get to the show on time they would have to leave immediately. Martin was disappointed when he learned that they had not all been seated together.

"Oh, what's the difference, we'll all see the same show," Margaret said. "Scotty and I will take the balcony, and if we lose each other in the crowd, we'll just take a cab and meet back at the apartment."

When they were seated, waiting for the curtain to rise, Angela showed signs of restlessness, squirming in her seat. But when the lights were lowered and the curtain rose for the first act she settled. She put her hand into Martin's and looked at him to see if he was concentrating on the performance. He wasn't and he looked right back at her.

"Do you like plays?" she asked.

"I've seen a few that I really enjoyed," he said. He could feel her pulse in her hand. She squeezed his hand intermittently and then dropped their held hands into her lap. There he could feel the warmth of her pubic area, and he could no longer concentrate on the performance.

After the show they could not find Margaret and Scotty, so they hailed a cab and headed back to the apartment in the Village.

"Hey, what a mob," Angela said, as she and Martin came into the room. "We couldn't even find you two at intermission. And what a show! Wasn't it really great?"

"Yes, it really is," answered Margaret.

"I couldn't help noticing the filthy language," Martin said. "But I guess it wouldn't be a New York play without that." When no one responded, he said: "What did you think, Scott?"

"It was O. K.," he answered.

"Well, what do you say,?" Margaret said, trying to change the subject. "Should we fix something to eat for these guys?" She moved toward the kitchen and Angela got up and followed her. Together they started getting out dishes and food.

"Hey, look at this," cried Angela. "These two have already had time to have a drink. You and Scotty must have been lucky getting a cab back here in such a hurry. What's the matter? Don't your other guests rate a drink?"

Margaret stopped in her tracks, realizing now that she had forgotten to put away the bottle and glasses.

"Oh, sure," she responded immediately. "Sure you rate a drink. I'm sorry. I didn't think of offering you a drink because Martin usually doesn't take one."

"Oh, he'll have a drink," said Angela. "Won't you, Martin? I've never met a sailor yet who wouldn't have a drink."

"No, thanks. I really don't care for any right now."

"Oh, come on, do a girl a favor. I don't like drinking alone, and I am thirsty right now," she said. "I'll fix them and I'll do it right. You'll enjoy it."

She fixed the drinks, then took them into the living room and handed one to Scotty and Martin. He learned previously that it was better to accept the first drink in such situations to avoid making a scene, then hanging on to it for the rest of the evening. He took the drink and sipped on it.

"Come on, Martin," said Angela shortly thereafter. "Let's bottoms-up on this one. I want to get back into the kitchen to help with dinner."

He looked at her thoughtfully for a moment. He felt an electrifying attraction as he engaged her eyes deeply with his own, and then he 'bottoms-upped' with her. He handed her his glass and thought that would be the end of it. But in a few minutes she returned with another drink.

"You can't stand on one leg," she said. "So here's for the other leg. Let's bottoms-up again. They really take hold when you do that."

She was right. They really did take hold, and believing this would be the final drink before dinner, he said: "O. K. bottoms up!"

Scotty had tuned in good dance music on the radio, and was sitting there at the other end of the room, still following Margaret's every move.

"You sure are quiet," Martin said to him, his words now slurred from the effects of the drink. "Don't you think this is better than the afternoon you had in mind.?"

"I'm beginin' to see your point," said Scotty. "In fact, I was just thinkin' maybe we could all spend the rest of the evenin' together--the four of us. What do you think of your date, I mean Angela?"

"She's O. K. She's interesting. Don't you think? She must be a nice girl or she wouldn't be a friend of Margaret's."

At that moment Angela's voice came from the kitchen, much too loudly. "Dinner is served. Come on, Sailors, chow down!"

Martin and Scotty both laughed and went to the table.

"It sounds like you've been in the company of sailors before," Martin said, smiling.

"Oh, yes," Angela answered. "My brother Frank has been in the Navy for over eight years. He graduated from the Naval Academy, he was on destroyers for a number of years, and now, my mother says, he was just recently made Executive Officer of some auxiliary ship. He's . . ."

"Did you say Frank, Frank Rosetto, Lieutenant Frank Rosetto?" Martin asked excitedly.

"Yeah, did you say Frank Rosetto?" echoed Scotty.

"Yes. Why?"

"He's on our ship," answered Martin. "He's our new Exec."

"It must be him," said Scotty. "Is he a sort of a average built guy with black hair?"

"Sounds like Frank," answered Angela. She was somewhat stunned by this revelation.

"It sure is a small world, as the saying goes," Martin said. "We haven't really talked to him as yet. The Captain announced that he was the new executive officer, and he has been all over the ship and up on the bridge, of course. But nobody in the deck gang has talked to him as yet, only the guys on the bridge."

"Sounds like Frank," Angela repeated. "I haven't seen or heard from him for several years. He writes my mother a couple of times a year, never mentions me. He doesn't approve of . . . well . . . we sort of had a fall-out a couple of years ago. We used to get along when we were children, but not in recent years. Actually he was an adopted son of my parents, about five years before I was born."

"Haven't your parents heard that he is at the Brooklyn Navy Yard, that his ship is there for repairs?" Scotty asked.

"They haven't mentioned it," Angela answered.

"They haven't?" Martin said, looking very confused.

"Hey, you guys," Margaret finally interjected. "Finish your dinner. The food is getting cold and the coffee is ready."

NINE

Nature's Irresistible Demands

After dinner Angela suggested they go dancing. "The Tango Club on Broadway has a very good dance band," she said.

"I like dancing," Scotty said.

"Sounds good to me," said Martin.

"Well, let's go then," said Margaret. "Time's fading fast away."

They left the apartment and headed for Broadway by taxi. The cab driver was very talkative. "You sailors must be having one helluva time in the Atlantic nowadays, right?"

At first, neither Martin nor Scotty answered. But finally Scotty said: "Yeah, some ships are having it rough with those German U-boats."

"Yeah, I've been hearing all about it on my radio for weeks, now. The Germans are sinking ships in those convoys to England hand over fist. I hear they are sinking hundreds of them. That's the word we get from down on the docks too. But now, since they tried to sink one of our destroyers, President Roosevelt gave the Navy the order to shoot on sight any German ship or sub they see in a certain area. That sounds like we're in a war to me. I don't know why he don't just call a spade a spade and declare war. We're in a war but the American people don't know it."

"Oh, that's all in the newspapers too," said Margaret. "That's all you see in the papers anymore. But, it's the Congress that has to declare war, isn't it?"

"I think so," said Martin. "But the President is the Commander-in-Chief of the Army and Navy, and he has a lot to do with getting the Congress to do it. I understand most American people don't want to get into war."

Martin remembered hearing about the destroyer USS GREER being attacked by U-boats while on convoy duty in the North Atlantic. He wondered then why with all the shipping activity going on in the Atlantic, his ship was being transferred to the Pacific.

"Yes," Angela said. "It's all such bad news that I don't even bother to read it anymore. Do you think we'll get into the war, Scotty?"

"Well, that's why I came back into the Navy. They ain't drafting all those men for nothin' you know. Sure we're gonna get into the war. The Germans ain't gonna let us alone as long as we are helping the English. That's what it looks like to me anyhow."

The taxi pulled up in front of the Tango Club, and the driver said: "Well, you kids have a good time and live it up while you can, you know the old saying, eat, drink, and be merry . . . "

The band was playing a popular swing tune as they entered the club, and the notes of a clarinet, drowning out the other instruments, hopped and skipped jazzily about the room. Most of the tables were in use and the center dance floor was crowded. The dancing couples were mostly of the younger set, with here and there a bald or slightly graying man having a good time dancing merrily with a younger partner.

Finally a waiter appeared at their table. "Let's have more bourbon and soda," Angela said. "If you drink the same thing all night, it will never bother you."

Martin gave a questioning look, but agreed. He was still feeling the drinks they had earlier.

He danced mostly with Angela. They talked very little while they danced, because Angela continually snuggled her face tightly against his shoulder and then sang the words to the song being played. She seemed to be in a trance, lost in the emotions called forth by the words and the music. Her voice was sweet and tender, like a little girl's voice.

Every now and again, while they danced, Angela would squeeze Martin's left hand, trying evidently, to convey some unspoken message to him. He enjoyed dancing. Angela danced gracefully and since there was little conversation between them, his thoughts often wandered to thoughts of Alice. He wished it could be Alice there with him and he pretended it was her there in his arms. Then he would come back to the present and realize he still did not know what he should do about her. Damn, he thought, I've got to do something about Alice.

Whenever he saw Scotty and Margaret, he noticed they were always talking, giving complete attention to, and engrossed in one another. They seemed not to be conscious of the others, and he wondered what they were talking about.

The evening passed rapidly and shortly after midnight they left the club. They stopped in a restaurant for coffee and a snack. While they waited to be served, it was decided that Martin and Scotty would spend the night at

Margaret's apartment and that Martin would take Angela home in a taxi while Scotty and Margaret went on ahead.

The couples parted when they left the restaurant. Martin and Angela immediately hailed a taxi and headed to her home in Queens.

"Should I have the cab wait for me?" Martin asked, as they pulled up in front of the tall brick home.

"I wouldn't," Angela replied. "There is an all-night taxi stand about two blocks from here. We can get a cab from our house in a few minutes most anytime."

The street was dark, having only small, dim street lights, and as they climbed the steps to the house, Martin noticed that there were no lights showing from any of the windows. Angela snapped on a dim table lamp as they entered the living room.

"We usually have a night cap around here. I hope you'll join me," she said.

"Oh, I don't know," Martin said. "I've had plenty already." He didn't want another drink, because he had already had more than he was accustomed to, and his head felt dull. Besides, Angela appeared to have had too much to drink. He could see that she was affected by the alcohol. Her eyes looked dreamy and she was unsteady when she walked. But without another word, she left the living room and returned in a few minutes carrying two drinks. She set them down on the coffee table, and sat down on the sofa.

"Come join me, Martin," she said, dreamily. "You look dejected. This drink will pep you up."

He immediately left the chair in which he had been sitting and joined her on the sofa. They drank together in silence, and she kept looking up at Martin smiling. It was a beautiful smile, and in the dim light that reflected ever so slightly on her moist lips, she was very pretty. But her head and shoulders swayed every now and again.

Finally, Angela moved closer to him. Her eyes captured his and held them. "You're a very strange fellow," she said. "You're not at all like your sister, Margaret. It's hard to believe you two are related."

"What do you mean by that?"

"Oh, I don't know exactly what I mean. It's no bad reflection on your sister. When I said that you were strange, I meant that you are, well, most of the other dates I have had, well, a lot of them were so fast and loose. You seem so gentle and, well, reserved."

Martin was somewhat embarrassed. "Do you live here with your folks?" he asked, trying to change the subject.

"Yes. My mother and dad are very old. They were old when I was born. They couldn't have any children when they were young, so they finally adopted Frank. Then five years later I came along when my mother was well past forty. By that time they weren't too happy about having a baby."

The change of subject somehow changed her mood. She slid her hand down into Martin's. "I have often wished my parents were younger. My home life has always seemed so different from that of my friends--old parents--an adopted older brother--it's not the same as-- sometimes it's awful." Her head swayed. Her speech slurred. Then she was silent.

"Let's not talk about me any more," she said finally, in a light-hearted way. "I've heard quite a lot about you from Margaret. I understand you were studying to be a minister. How come you joined the Navy as an enlisted man? That seems like such a big switch."

"Well, Angela, at this point, I'm not quite sure. I've asked myself that question quite often lately. I just had an idea that a year in the Navy would do me some good. It's a long story." He became silent and his thoughts drifted again to the fight with Jim Johnson, there was something bothering him about that. Something wasn't right about it, something didn't fit. But the remembrance of it brought on the awful, overpowering feelings of remorse and guilt. Then, shaking off those thoughts, he continued. "I guess I was really in some kind of an emotional crisis, sorta like being at the crossroad and not knowing which way to go. I started out really wanting to be a minister, and it would have been so easy. Four years of college, then the Lutheran seminary, then a church. But the more I studied, the more I listened and learned, the harder it became to believe what I was learning and what I would be expected to teach. I wanted to believe. Oh, yes, I really wanted to believe, but there were always these lingering doubts. What I was consciously agreeing with, on the surface, deeper down inside of me, I was rejecting. It was as if my head was saying one thing and my heart something else; you know, like the difference between thinking something and feeling something. Oh, I'm sorry , this must be boring. I guess it's the drink that's making me talk. You don't want to hear this."

"No, don't stop, please go on," Angela said tenderly.

"Well, I had to believe, if I wanted to become a Christian minister and teach and preach the Christian religion. But I kept having these doubts, especially about the birth and death of Jesus. It all seemed so illogical. It just didn't fit in with anything I knew to be possible, and those stories just didn't answer the questions I had about God. There was just no proof. I tell you sincerely, I really wanted to believe it all, because I wanted to be a minister. But how could I? There were so many things that just didn't make any sense. For instance, like Jesus being missing from the grave and he had risen, bodily, from the grave and went up into heaven. Oh, I know this was probably meant to be metaphoric, it is a symbolic, two thousand year old myth. But they are not teaching it that way, and this bothers me, if you know what I mean."

"I do believe in many of the things that Jesus taught about how to live in harmony with our fellow man. Like, 'loving our neighbors as ourselves,' or like, 'turning the other cheek,' and that sort of thing, but so much of the rest of it just seems to be the church's rationalization in order to make a complete story. And now, two thousand years later, how do we know how much was added to the story, and what was omitted."

"What you're saying, is that you've lost your faith."

"Oh, no, no, please don't misunderstand me. I have faith. I have faith in mankind, in my fellow man, in people, and I have faith in God. The problem is, how I perceive God. Who is God? What is God. What is God like? My perception of God is not the same as the church's description. I know that is a problem, for me. But I just can't bring myself to believe that God is some supremely, perfect personal Being, who is also both transcendent and immanent, and beyond human understanding. I have a feeling that God is somewhat closer to having human attributes. That's what I feel most strongly. I think maybe that is what Jesus was trying to teach when he said that

God is like a father. But the church says that we must accept its doctrine on faith, and that faith is the abandonment of our own dependence on ourselves, on our own security, and that we must put our trust in a 'God in Three Persons' which is one God. It's all so confusing, Angela. But, look, I'm sorry, I guess I never really put that into words before. The drink got to me I guess, and I'm thinking out loud something I haven't been able to express before. You must think . . . "

"Yeah, you really are a strange fellow," Angela said, smiling. "But I can understand why you gave it up and joined the Navy. I didn't know the Christian religion could be so complicated. I never think too much about it. I try never to question anything about the church, that's for the church fathers to worry about. I'm a Catholic because I was born a Catholic. But I'm not a very devout Catholic. I go to mass, sometimes, and to confession, which can be a good thing, 'specially when you've done something really bad, well . . ."

"I have the highest respect for Catholicism," said Martin.

"By that you probably mean the Catholic church and all Catholics in general. But how about one real live Catholic girl?" Angela moved closer to Martin, put her arm around his shoulder and her head on his chest. For a moment, just a fleeting moment, he could have sworn that Alice was there beside him; and in that fleeting moment, the old, haunting thoughts flashed into his mind again. He realized now he was feeling the same aching, longing desire to possess this girl sitting there beside him, and suddenly he understood what Alice was trying to tell him in her letter.

Instinctively he put his arms around Angela and held her tightly. But then, he stood up abruptly. He picked up his hat.

"I think I better get going," he said.

"Why?" Angela asked, stunned by his sudden change of attitude.

He looked down at her. He did not know what to say. In her eyes he saw now what seemed to be the expression of a child who had just been scolded, and refused something which it urgently wanted. He hesitantly walked over to the door.

Angela rushed over to him on slightly unsteady legs. "Don't go now," she cried, bursting into tears. "I need you. I really need you." She threw her arms around his body and dropped to her knees in front of him. She opened the flap of his bell-bottomed trousers and they slipped down with his shorts to the floor. In seconds he dropped to the floor with her in sheer ecstasy. Together, with four hands, they frantically removed her clothing, and then they blended together and became one in obedience to nature's irresistible demands.

Afterwards they sat on the sofa to finish their drinks. They touched each other tenderly and acknowledged, through each other's eyes, the understanding that two people can have only through the experience they had just had together. And again, Martin felt that sense of loss which was in reality an expansion of the circle of his knowledge, and an awareness of the fact that a return to the smaller circle of innocence was forever impossible.

Wrapped in each others arms, they fell asleep.

TEN

Parting's Sweet Sorrow

The quietness of the night was broken by the rattling of milk bottles as the milkman made his early morning deliveries. It was 5:00 A. M. Martin woke up wondering momentarily where he was, and as soon as he moved, Angela also awoke. She smiled and yawned. He tried to stretch his legs and move out of the contorted position they had gotten themselves into on the sofa as they slept. Then he rose and began to smooth down his hair with his hands and arrange his clothing.

"I better get going," he said. "I want to get back to see Margaret before we go back aboard the ship." He walked to the outside door. Angela followed him. When he put his hand on the door knob and the latch clicked, she threw her arms around his neck.

"Martin," she whispered, "will we ever see each other again?"

"I don't know," Martin answered, thoughtfully. "I'll most likely have liberty again the day after tomorrow. I'll call you as soon as I get ashore. In the meantime, I'll be thinking of you every minute." He put his arms around her and held her tightly as they kissed a long good-bye. But Angela apparently sensed the rekindled sexual fire burning between them, and she pulled away from him.

"I'll probably never see you again," she said.

"Why do you say that? I want to see you again."

"Because I'm Italian and you're not, and because you're in the Navy," she said.

"Does it matter to you that I'm not Italian?" Martin asked.

"No, no, not to me," she said. "But it does to my parents and it probably does to you. And, oh, I don't know why we are discussing this."

But Martin wasn't listening to her words. The gates had been opened. The animal which had been pent up inside him, had now been set free. Like a stallion, Martin was able to pursue his mate, unrestricted. And together they cast off all the inhibitions, all of the taboos, all of the religious restraints and all of the sensible rules of civilized behavior, and they made love in a manner that bordered on mutual ravishment. They hastily and clumsily helped remove each other's clothing. They spread the articles of clothing on the living room floor and used them as a love nest.

"Let's quiet down," said Angela. "If we wake up my parents, we'll be in big trouble."

They simmered down. They prolonged the mutual pleasure as long as they could. And then they finished with the deepest and most satisfying experience either of them had ever known.

Afterwards, Martin said, "Angela, I used to dream that there was a woman in the world like you, and I used to dream that I was making love to that woman. But I knew it was a dream. I knew it was just fantasy. But, Angela, you are real, and I'm real, and we are here in the real world, and it is a much larger world now than I ever imagined it could be. So you're Italian, and your Catholic, and you have customs and beliefs which are different from mine and the Protestant girls I have known. So what? I don't know about you, but I know this: I love you, Angela. I love you like I've never loved before. I'll always love you. But I must go now. I'll be back to see you as soon as possible. Good-bye for now."

"Good-bye, Martin," she said, as her face twisted in anguish, and tears rolled down her cheeks.

Martin pulled her into his arms again and kissed her wet cheeks, and upon seeing that painful countenance he felt the weight of the commitment he had just made. Then he walked out and closed the door behind him. He hurried down the street toward the taxi stand, feeling taller and stronger and more courageous than he had ever felt before. He felt the power of being a man.

When he got back to Margaret's apartment, he found Scotty had removed his jumper and shoes. Margaret was wearing lounging pajamas and a robe. The scene was one of intimacy, and Martin felt like an intruder.

"You're just in time for breakfast," said Margaret. "We were beginning to get worried about you. I wasn't going to wait much longer before calling Angela. I probably would have called sooner, but Scotty said he knew you would be O. K. You and Ange must have hit it off real well. Right?"

"Yes. She's a very nice girl, very nice. I really like her."

"Well, move over, Alice!" Margaret said jovially.

"Yeah," said Martin. "I haven't answered Alice's letter as yet, but now I can do it." He realized now the problem had been resolved through the new insight he had gained from the experience he'd had with Angela. He understood

Alice's decision now, and he would write her at the first opportunity. It was no longer a dilemma.

"You sound like you're gettin' over it," said Scotty. "You shoulda seen him when he first got that letter, Margaret. I thought sure he was goin' to jump overboard. But I didn't blame him. From her picture, Alice looks like a really neat woman."

"Well, I was shocked to hear what she had done. I thought Alice was a very nice person, and she and Martin seemed to be so much love. But, as they say, 'that's life.'"

Scotty went into the bedroom, and then came back later fully dressed.

"I love those dress-blue Navy uniforms," said Margaret.

"Yes," Martin said, looking down at himself. "They're practical and they don't look bad. I'll go freshen up, then we better get back to the ship. What do you say, Scotty?"

"Right. We might as well leave in good time. We don't want to be AOL and get restricted while we're in New York, that's for sure."

"That's for sure!" Martin said, thinking of Angela.

When they were ready to leave, Martin gave his sister a quick brotherly kiss. "Thanks for everything," he said. "I promised to call Angela on our next liberty. Maybe I could pick her up on the way and then stop over here again, if that's O. K. I'll call and let you know."

"Sure," she said. "And you come too, Scotty."

Scotty agreed, and as they left he and Margaret lingered an embarrassingly long time at the apartment door. Martin was kept waiting in the taxi, with the meter running, but he didn't say anything when Scotty finally came out and climbed into the cab. They were both silent as they headed back to the Brooklyn Navy Yard.

The following day Martin had the duty as he expected. He had a four hour watch as a lookout on the bridge, which was monotonous because there was very little activity after the liberty party left for the day. The only activity was back on the fantail, on the main deck. They were in dock, he learned, not for engine repairs, but for the installation of depth charge launchers, requiring only a couple of special technical personnel from the Navy Yard and a couple of their own deck hands and machinist's mates.

During his off duty hours he went to the mess hall to write the letter which he had resolved he would write to Alice. The letter was as follows:

Dear Alice,

It was not easy to get over the effects of your shocking letter, as you undoubtedly expected. I just never thought that the relationship we had built up over a period of four years could end so abruptly. Of course I realize now that I am as much to blame as you are that it ended this way.

At first I didn't think I would ever understand how it came about or that I would ever get over it. But I did get over it. And I've had several experiences in the past few weeks that have helped me to understand your situation, and your decision. I won't go into the details at this time.

I'm sure I could not explain it as accurately and in as much detail as you did in your letter.

I guess our relationship was, after all, just a college relationship which had to end with graduation. At any rate my mother has a saying, "Everything happens for the best." I sincerely hope your decision will turn out "the best" for you and for everyone affected by your decision.

What more can I say? I wish you much happiness in your new life.

Sincerely yours,

Martin

He read over the letter and knew that it was not completely truthful. He felt the sadness and the sense of loss, and knew that he couldn't just write off their relationship with such casualness and such callousness. In spite of all that had happened, he still loved Alice. Theirs had been a true-love relationship. They had spent many days and months and years together. They had studied together and had taken required courses together. They had many long philosophical discussions, and they shared many views of the world. He knew that he could not end that relationship as easily as his letter indicated, and he had not really gotten over Alice's sudden decision to take up with another man. But the partial truth in his letter was that since his experience with Angela, he was making progress toward getting over it.

The following Monday morning, immediately after all hands had returned from liberty at 0900, the Executive Officer announced that there would be no liberty for the day and that they would be preparing to get underway later in the day.

This was another surprise. The scuttlebutt was that they had to join a convoy and act as an escort vessel because of increased German U-boat activity off the Atlantic coast. It was also another new adventure he could look forward to in the days ahead. It was also a great disap-

pointment. He had looked forward with such great anticipation to seeing Angela again. She had expressed the
premonition that they might never see each other again,
but he could not allow this to happen.

A plan formed in his mind. With newly found initiative, he dashed up to the wardroom area, in officer's country, and found the Executive Officer's cabin. He knocked
on the door.

"Who's there?" said a voice from inside.

"It's Martin Miller, from the deck gang, Sir," he said.
"May I speak with Lieutenant Frank Rosetto?"

The door opened and standing there in his shorts,
holding the door, was a medium built, dark, hairy man.
He looked at Martin somewhat in amazement. "What do
you want? I'm in a hurry to get dressed. I have to get
ashore and back before we prepare to get underway." He
seemed almost apologetic.

"Begging your pardon, Sir," said Martin. "I have a personal problem, Sir, I thought you might help me with."

"Do you have your Chief's permission to be up here?"
the Lieutenant asked, noting Martin's Seaman Second
Class rating. "Can't this wait until later? I'm really in a
hurry."

"No, Sir," Martin answered quickly. "You see, Sir, I met
your sister, Angela, on Saturday, and I promised to see her
again before we shove off. But I didn't know we were going to leave so soon."

"I didn't either," the Executive Officer answered. "Step
in here a minute. How did you meet my sister?"

"Well, Sir, she's a friend of my sister, my sister, Margaret, who lives here in Greenwich Village. I met her Saturday night at my sister's apartment and I want to see her

again before we leave. I thought maybe you could give me special permission to go ashore for a couple of hours. I'm off duty until 1800 tonight."

"Hold on a minute, Miller," he said, as he continued dressing. "Look, I haven't been ashore myself as yet since we're here in Brooklyn. I had to take command of the ship while it is in dock, because the Captain took off for a couple of days to see his family. I haven't seen my parents in over three years and they live right here in Queens."

"I know, Sir, I was at your parent's home Saturday night. I took Angela home."

"Well, look, requests for special shore leave must be made through your Division Chief, then they come to me for approval. But, look, I'm going ashore very shortly. I have a Navy car waiting for me. You go see your Chief to fill out a chit for special liberty, then you can ride along with me. We'll have to be back on board in about four hours. Did you meet my parents?"

"No, Sir," Martin said, then added, "it was late."

It had worked. The Chief eyed him suspiciously when Martin requested the special liberty to go ashore with the Executive Officer, but he signed the liberty chit without comment. Like Scotty had said, he was a good chief.

Martin was waiting when Lieutenant Rosetto rushed up to the Navy car, a gray, 1939 Plymouth sedan. He had chosen to drive himself and he wasted no time leaving the Navy Yard, heading toward his home.

"Lieutenant, I just remembered that Angela will be working today." Martin said. "She and my sister work for the same company, that's how they became friends. I'm sure she'll be working until five o'clock, 1700 hours, I mean, and you said you had to be back on board before that time."

"Oh, man! You should have mentioned that before. But, O. K., look, I'll drive to my parent's home, then you take the car and drive downtown and go see her," said Rosetto, with obvious disgust.

"Aye, aye, Sir." Martin answered. "But you won't get to see her then."

"Like I said before, I haven't seen my parents for over three years and besides, Angela and I haven't talked much for the past several years. She and I have some major differences of opinion, mostly regarding family matters. Look, Miller, you just go see her and you give her my regards. We don't have enough time, and whatever you do, you make sure you get back to my parent's house by 1500 hours, three o'clock. I want to get back aboard by 1600."

"Aye, aye, Sir," Martin answered. He had some reservations about driving in downtown New York, but as soon as Rosetto got out of the car in front of the house, he slipped behind the wheel and was soon speeding across the bridge to Manhattan.

Angela and Margaret were just leaving for lunch when Martin walked into the lobby of the petroleum company where they both worked as private secretaries. He was thrilled, he was ecstatic as he watched them approach and saw the rhythmic swaying of Angela's lithe, slender body and the long, black hair reaching almost to her hips. She was beautiful, just beautiful and his pulse rate quickened when she drew near.

"What a surprise!" Angela exclaimed. "What brings you here at this odd time?"

Margaret said much the same and was surprised at the familiarity and the intimacy with which Martin and Angela greeted one another.

Martin explained the circumstances. "I don't know how I got so lucky to have your brother help me get to see you. He probably thinks I'm a real nuisance. But, Angela, I had to see you just one more time before we leave."

"Wow, you two really fell hard, didn't you?" Margaret said.

"I guess we can't deny it," said Martin. "Nothing like this ever happened to me before."

Angela looked up into his eyes and he could see that she was very pleased. "Nor me," she said, smiling broadly.

"Your friend Scotty and I got fairly well acquainted too," Margaret said with a touch of mysteriousness in her tone.

"I noticed that," Martin said. "It's too bad, but he had the duty and won't be allowed off the ship."

The three of them had lunch at a nearby restaurant. After lunch it was time for Martin to start back. He said good-bye to Margaret. Angela insisted on going along to see her brother Frank and she wanted Martin to meet her parents. So, after some delay, she got permission to take the afternoon off. Martin told her that his ship would be transferred to the Pacific Fleet and that it might be a long time until he would see her again.

"I knew it. I just knew it," she said angrily. "That's the way it always is with you sailors. Any girl is a fool to get interested in a sailor."

Back at the Rosetto home, the introductions to her parents were awkward and somewhat embarrassing. Martin overheard Angela's mother whisper to her father, "Oh,

dear, another one." He wondered what she meant by that.
Her father opened a bottle of his favorite wine and poured
for everyone.

"I heard you two coming home last night," he said. "But
I didn't hear you leave. I fell asleep. I hope you went
home at a decent time."

Martin's face flushed and he stuttered, "I, I, my mo,
mother wouldn't think it was a decent time."

Her father laughed and seemed to appreciate the hu-
mor. The meeting between Angela and her brother was
also awkward, but it seemed they were both happy it took
place.

"Thanks for coming home to see me," Frank said.

"Thanks for making it possible," Angela returned.

Martin sensed that there was a complete new set of relationships opening up here which had not existed before
and that each of their futures would somehow be affected
by these new relationships. When the time came for them
to part, Martin and Angela, in the presence of the family,
embraced and clung to one another desperately for a long
moment, as if they were parting forever. He pulled away,
and walked out of the house toward the gray Navy car.
He stretched himself to his full six foot height before getting into the car. He felt again a new strength and courage
surging through him, but he did not know at this time the
depth nor the heights he was to reach as the aftermath of
this unusual but brief encounter with a truly lovable, loving woman. For there had been unleashed the wild, turbulent force within him, and it would whirl and rage un-
abated for a long time before it was finally tamed and
spent.

ELEVEN

The Horns of Dilemma

As they left the Brooklyn Navy Yard, Martin saw that the USS FLEET TUG was being maneuvered into line with several other ships, heading toward the mouth of the Hudson bay, where they were to rendezvous with additional ships. Off in the distance to starboard he could see the Statue of Liberty. He was thrilled as the sight of it evoked in him an awareness of his citizenship in the greatest land of liberty and freedom in the world, the United States of America. He was proud of that and also proud to be serving in its great Navy. They were in line behind two old oil tankers and far up ahead was a newly refurbished destroyer, proudly leading the way.

Scotty and Martin were working along with other seamen of the deck force, cleaning up the areas where the depth-charge launchers were installed.

"Where do you think we are going?" Martin asked.

"I don't know," Scotty answered. "I hear that the ships' captains got new orders that they are supposed to keep their ports of call secret now, because there are too many German spies around finding out where and when our ships are sailing, and then, Pow! They're sunk by the German U-boats. Let's ask the Chief."

They were working on the fantail of the ship. Scotty crossed over to the port side and approached the Chief Boatswain's Mate, Harry McCroye.

"Where do you think we're headed, Chief?" asked Scotty.

"I don't know," the Chief answered. "I didn't hear the official word yet. But it looks to me as if we are going to play escort to some of them old tankers." The ships were now heading out into the open sea. "According to the way those tankers are taking up positions," the Chief continued as he studied them, "I'd say we're going to take a south-easterly course. That means Cuba or Puerto Rico. Those tankers are loaded, but I don't know why they'd be going there. I'll get the official dope from the guys on the bridge, and I'll let you know as soon as I find out." Martin was happy to hear what McCroye had said. For the prospect of traveling to any of the ports mentioned filled him with excitement. He was anxious to see more of the world which he learned about in geography books.

The next day while he and Scotty and several other seamen were busy painting bulkheads below decks, Martin began to feel the uselessness of doing this kind of manual work. It became to him worse than the type of work that had bored him in his father's plant during summer vacations. He decided he must do something about this situation, so he spoke with Chief McCroye.

"I'll see what I can do," the Chief had said, rather reluctantly. But soon afterwards, he called Martin aside. "I spoke with Lieutenant Rosetto, who seems to be your friend. We are starting a new training program and you'll be assigned to do duty on the bridge as the Captain's talker."

"What will I be doing when I'm on watch?" Martin asked.

"You just see that you are there to relieve the watch on time, stay awake and do what you are instructed. You'll be taught what to do. You'll be handling the Captain's communications internally on board the ship whenever you are on watch and the ship is underway. They'll teach you how to do it."

It was exciting to think that he would be on the bridge where the Captain spent most of his time and where there were always other officers present. Martin looked forward to this new assignment with anticipation. "That sounds great," he said. "Thank you, Sir."

"Don't Sir me!" McCroye roared.

"Well, O. K., then," Martin returned, humiliated and surprised by the Chief's outburst.

"And if you want to learn to be a sailor, don't use O.K. either. Aye, aye, is what you use aboard ship." Then he added, "Your first watch will be the twelve noon to 1600 hours and then midnight to 0400," and he strutted off to another part of the ship.

"I'm not sure if the Chief likes me or not," Martin said after he rejoined Scotty.

"Aw, don't worry about it," Scotty said. "He's probably a little mad because you'll be doing less work on the deck gang if you get duty on the bridge. But don't worry about him. You find guys like that on every ship. They've got a lot of bark, but hearts as big as gold, and not much bite. Just do what he tells you, and let the rest go in one ear and out the other. I still think McCroye is a pretty good chief."

The afternoon watch that day Martin found to be very uneventful. However, it gave him an opportunity to view from the bridge the entire convoy as it steamed along in formation. The six oil tankers were in the center, in rows, two by two, and one old four-stacker destroyer up ahead on the starboard flank and one of the newer class destroyers on the port, as escorts. Up ahead of them, leading the way was the other four-stacker. Their own fleet tug brought up the rear. "I suppose we are along to pick up any of those old tankers in case they conk out," one of the quartermasters on the bridge said to Martin. "In fact, the way they look to me, we'll probably have to take them all in tow before we get to wherever we're going."

Martin thought of asking, "Where are we going?" But since it was his first watch on the bridge he thought better of it. It was interesting and informative. He learned to use the voice-powered speakers and ear phones while wearing a special steel helmet.

On the second day, one of the signalmen on the bridge said, "We're off of Cape Hatteras right now, and we are lucky we've got such a calm sea. The weather is usually rough as hell when you're off the coast of Cape Hatteras."

It appeared to be another calm day. But just as Martin was relieving the watch again at midnight, the Captain was shouting to the Chief Quartermaster: "Get that position plotted right. I don't think the damn Group Commander is going to pay any attention to the storm warning. We may have to steer our own course."

During the afternoon and evening the sea had become steadily more active. And now, from up there on the bridge, Martin could see the convoy traveling in a southwardly direction, still in formation, but at a slower speed. The seas were getting heavier and the wind velocity was increasing.

The O. D. reported to the Captain that the barometer had taken an unusual drop, and the Captain gave orders to bog-down from stem to stern. A few minutes later word was received from a shore station along the coast that the main force of a hurricane had suddenly changed direction and was heading directly for the convoy. But only a short time after the message was received, the storm, in all its ungodly fury, was upon them. It seemed to Martin as if, while walking along in peaceful broad daylight someone, without warning, had flung a blanket over his head and then tossed, tumbled and dragged him all over the rough countryside.

There were mighty gusts of wind. There were waves ranging from thirty to fifty feet high, some of which they floated over and others which the fleet tug ploughed through like a submarine. It seemed as if their ship lay completely on one side and then on the other. Martin and his shipmates sometimes sat on the bulkheads of the bridge as if they were slanted decks.

When Martin was relieved of his watch and was trying to cross from one side of the mess hall to the other, he slipped on the water drenched steel deck and was flung head first against a steel hatchway on the other side. Weak from the impact of flesh against steel, he reached out for the leg of a stationary table. But before he could grab hold of it, the ship lurched in the opposite direction and he slid, like a toppled ski jumper, on his back, across the mess hall deck. Then while the ship lay momentarily on the side to which he had descended, a shipmate grabbed hold of him and held him until he had regained his balance. Then, beaten and bruised, he made his way painfully down to the deck below to the crew's quarters. There, with much effort, he managed to climb into his bunk and strap himself into it with the elastic bunk straps.

For most of the crew this was the worst storm they had ever experienced, just as it was for Martin. He became extremely sea-sick, as many of the others did. They were all hungry, there was no possibility of preparing food, and yet the thought of food was repulsive. There was little conversation among the crew as the ship heaved and rolled through the long night. Each man had his own thoughts and for Martin it was a night of terror. Would the ship be able to ride it out? How long could such a storm last? Where were the other ships? Were they widely separated or were they so close that at any moment one of them would bear down upon the seaworthy tug and send it to the bottom? Wonder how Mother and Dad are? What the hell ever made me think I wanted to be a sailor? Will I ever see Angela again? Then, the black feelings of guilt came upon him again--the guilt of Jim Johnson's death. Overwhelming remorse enveloped him. Why did Jim Johnson have to die? He hadn't really hit him that hard. What was the strange look he had had on his face? Was he to live the rest of his life haunted by this memory? "Almighty God, my heavenly father," he said, speaking introvertedly, as if he were addressing an indwelling being deep within himself. "Forgive me. Will God forgive me?" For an instant he thought he was getting a response, almost like a voice starting to say something, but just then the ship lurched and the message was broken.

He became aware again of his surroundings. He tried to go to sleep, but he could not. The heaving of the ship caused his body to shift suddenly from one end of the bunk to the other and he had to hang on to the metal rails with both hands. The ship's sudden drops into seemingly bottomless pits would leave him suspended in midair. The elastic bunk straps stretched to their limit and his stomach felt as if it would tear loose from the rest of his body. His bunk was adjacent to the ship's hull and when the water smashed against the hull he could picture what it would be like if that part of the hull would suddenly cave in.

It was useless trying to stay in his bunk, so he worked his way back up to the mess hall. He looked out of one of the portholes but he could see nothing but water; no sky, no horizon, just water. He thought about Angela again. How delicious she was!

The storm continued all the next day and through the following night. But their sturdy vessel, by some miracle, was able to resist each of that killcrazy storm's murderous onslaughts. For cn the morning of the third day the storm receded as suddenly as it had come upon them. The other ships had scattered in all directions, but within the next two days they all regained their positions in the formation and they steamed ahead southwardly, steering a steady course.

"We're headed for Guantanamo Bay, Cuba," Chief Mc-Croye finally ventured. "We drop off these tankers there and then head for Panama. I just got the official word."

"Do we get to go ashore in Guantanamo Bay?" Scotty asked.

"No soap. Not in Guantanamo. We drop these tankers off and then take right off for the Panama Canal, and believe me, there are good liberty towns in Panama."

The rest of the voyage could have been like a vacation cruise except for the constant drills and training sessions.

The Caribbean Sea was tame and placid, with hardly a ripple on the water's surface. Martin marveled at the calmness and enjoyed being aboard the sturdy craft cutting through the water like a rich man's yacht.

Martin's watches on the bridge, as Captain's talker, often coincided with Lieutenant Rosetto's schedule. In addition to being Executive Officer, Rosetto was also the ship's navigator. He spent many hours on the bridge. During these times, Martin and Rosetto became better acquainted through long conversations in which they exchanged information about their backgrounds. Even though there was no obvious attempt to fraternize with an enlisted man, Martin knew it was more than official interest on the part of the Executive Officer. He assumed that this interest stemmed from the fact of his own friendship, or relationship with Angela. But he also knew that Rosetto demonstrated genuine friendship.

In one of those conversations he had said: "I suppose Angela mentioned that I'm an adopted son, she usually does."

"Yes, she did mention that."

"I figured as much. I guess Angela hasn't been the same since we found out about that. Some cousin of ours, or hers, told her about it in school one day, and when she came home she hounded my parents until they broke down and told us the story. Apparently my real mother got pregnant by her boyfriend, who was from a prominent Jewish family from Brooklyn. Well, his parents didn't want him to marry an Italian girl, and to make a long story short, they paid well to have the baby, me, put up for adoption. My real mother and my adopted mother, Mrs. Rosetto, had been girlfriends since their school days in

Brooklyn, so when the Rosettos' heard that their friend's baby was up for adoption, they jumped at the chance to adopt me, because they had been trying to get pregnant for a couple of years without success. Then Angela came along five years later. Everything seemed to change after she was born. I'll tell you about it some other time. I see it's time to relieve the watch."

The days of their cruise through the Caribbean waters enroute to Panama, though uneventful, were also satisfying for Martin in other ways. For during those days he was able to start into motion the chain of events which he hoped would eventually resolve the most pressing problem in his life. He simply could not do what Scotty, intending to be helpful, had recommended: "Forget it and don't say nothin' to nobody, 'cause there ain't nobody that can prove you had anything to do with Jim Johnson's death." He could not bury the feelings of guilt, remorse and self-condemnation that kept emerging from the subconscious conviction that he had broken the commandment, "Thou shalt not kill." It became an obsession that haunted him whenever his thoughts were not occupied elsewhere. It was beginning to wear on him both physically and mentally, and he knew he had to do something about it. Therefore he began to deliberately concentrate his thoughts and prayers on the problem, reviewing mentally all of the details again and again.

"What's the problem, Mart, you got the clap or something?" Scotty said to him one night after the evening meal. "You don't look right or act right lately."

"It's the same old problem, Scotty," he answered.

"Aw, why don't you forget that? You're just hurting yourself."

"It isn't that easy for me."

Then, as if in answer to his prayers, one night while he was engaged in deep concentration on the subject, he suddenly remembered again the strange look on Johnson's face just before he hit him the last time. There was something different about that look. Martin tried to fathom its meaning. It was as if Johnson had been trying to tell Martin something with the expression in his eyes. But what was it? He had not expected to beat Johnson that easily. That easily! That was it. It was too easy, much too easy. You don't beat a man like Johnson that easily unless he has some other kind of problem, something else interfering. There must have been something else. What was it? What was that look on his face? Was it pleading? Was it that he was trying to say, "Look, Martin, I can't back down because I have a reputation to live up to. I'm bigger than you and tougher than you. But, look, I'm having trouble. There's something wrong with me, but I can't back down, so go easy, I'm in trouble."

That's what the look on Johnson's face meant, that's what he was trying to say. Martin remembered the feeling he had in his arms and hands. He remembered holding back, as angry as he was and as hard as he was hitting, he was also at the same time pulling the punches. The picture of Johnson's face became clear to him in minute detail. He was having some kind of attack, but was trying to ignore it. He saw the look again in his mind's eye, and he knew he had the answer. Johnson was probably having a heart attack right then and there, in the restaurant.

This revelation was like a great and sudden relief. Every bone in his body, every muscle, every nerve felt this great relief from the sure knowledge that it was not he who had killed Jim Johnson. All that remained now was to confirm it, to verify it for his own satisfaction.

"Oh, thank God, thank you God," Martin shouted.

The seaman in the next bunk raised his head to see what was going on. "What the hell's ailin' you, Miller," he said.

Martin didn't answer. He left the crew's quarters and went looking for the Executive Officer, Frank Rosetto. He found him alone in the wardroom, reading.

"Excuse me, Lieutenant," Martin said. "I have another problem I would like to discuss with you, Sir."

"Sure, sure," he replied. "I meant it when I said my door is always open. We can talk here. All of the off-duty officers are in bed." He seemed genuinely pleased that Martin had come to see him.

"It's a fairly long story," Martin said. "But, I need your advice. Can this be strictly personal and confidential?"

"Certainly, Martin, we can talk privately here. If someone should come in we'll just switch the conversation to the subject of navigation. You mentioned you would like to learn navigation. What's on your mind?"

Martin told him all about the incident in Norfolk that fateful night when Jim Johnson died. He told him about the events that had preceded it. He also told him frankly of his troubled conscience and about the revelation he had just had that prompted him to seek Rosetto's counsel.

They talked long into the night. Rosetto asked many relevant questions, as Martin unfolded his involvement, and at one point he exclaimed, "Damn, this gives me a helluva conflict of interest. As Executive Officer I'm obligated to make an official report of this information. But I did give you my word that this conversation would be confidential."

Martin was therefore surprised when Rosetto gave him his first advice: "The official report of Johnson's death, from the Norfolk Naval Hospital to the Commanding Officer of this ship was that his death was due to injuries received in a free-for-all fight in Norfolk with persons unknown. Therefore, since there appears that there is no way you can be implicated, offhand, I would say the best course would be for you to do nothing. Just try to forget it. You're probably right that it was a heart attack, and you are not at fault.

But this would leave the problem unresolved. Rosetto's advice was the same as Scotty's and as Martin was shaking his head, indicating this was unacceptable, Rosetto continued, "But if you'd like to know, in order to clear your conscience, I can make some discreet inquiries through friends of mine in Norfolk. Maybe there was an autopsy or maybe we can get one."

"I sure wish you'd do that for me," Martin said.

"O. K., I'll get some letters off as soon as we arrive in Panama. I'll let you know as soon as I hear something."

"Thanks, Lieutenant," Martin said. He extended his hand in heartfelt appreciation, convinced that he had finally done the right thing to absolve himself of the blame for Jim Johnson's death.

Rosetto looked Martin directly in the eye and grasped his hand. "I hope I've been some help," he said.

TWELVE

Temptation and Stark Reality

From his vantage point on the bridge, the approach to the Panama Canal was exciting for Martin. They steamed past the breakwaters and through the approach channels into Limon Bay, and thence into Colon Harbor, while the heavy gray fog of early morning still surrounded them. The powerful, stubby gray vessel weaved its way in and around ships of all descriptions, steaming southward toward the locks. Then they were taken in tow by the "electric mules," special towing locomotives and guided into the first of the Gatun Locks, and then raised slowly and monotonously upward with the rising water.

Martin was struck by the difference between what he thought they would be like, from the descriptions he read in geography books, and what they were here in reality. From those descriptions of the prolonged struggle of the men who had built these locks and the canal, he had imagined them to be much more than what they appeared to be. He thought they would be larger. But he could not appreciate from looking at the finished product, all of the sweat, toil and struggle against immeasurable odds, or the cost of human energy that had gone into the making of this truly gigantic project.

The ascent through the various locks up to the last one seemed like it would go on forever, but at last they were through them and were once again steaming under their own power into the beautiful Gatun Lakes.

It was a new experience to be cruising on inland waters. The powerful fleet tug sprinted along like a young stallion let loose after having been stabled for the winter. This leg of the journey through the Isthmus of Panama went by quickly. He stood watch on the bridge and was thrilled by the beauty that now surrounded them. He thought again of Angela and of the events which took place back in New York. He felt now like a man of the world, and he was pleased by the new courage and self-confidence he was feeling. He was glad he joined the Navy.

In due time, however, the beauty of the Gatun Lakes could only be seen in the dim view behind them, and they proceeded through the narrow Culebra Cut which sliced jaggedly through the earth's crust, not unlike the trail of a rambling little natural river. In spots it cut through fields which almost seemed familiar, and then again through the heavy jungle-like underbrush that brought to mind the history book pictures of the gigantic struggle of its builders against all of the obstacles which nature had imposed.

Then, being lifted up once more by the Pedro Miguel Lock, before long they were lowered to the Pacific tidewater by the Miraflores Locks from which they steamed into the Bay of Panama and thence to the port of Balboa. Here the USS FLEET TUG tied up alongside one of the port's huge piers to take on much needed supplies.

Two thirds of the ship's officers and men were granted liberty to go ashore in Panama City until midnight, 2400 hours Martin and Scotty were included in this first liberty party. It was their first time ashore since they left New York, and Martin felt as if he had been a prisoner and was now stepping out into freedom for the first time. His spirits were high, and now in addition, being in a foreign country for the first time in his life, he was aflame with curiosity.

He and Scotty decided they would tour Panama City together. They walked into town and as they drew further away from the docks and entered the city, Martin could feel the excitement welling up inside of him. Scotty evidently shared his mood, for they walked along swiftly in silence.

When they reached the heart of the city with its strange, quaint buildings and narrow streets, Martin noted particularly the unusual mixture of people. Some were Spaniards, others Indians, some white, some black. There were the countless numbers who were such a mix that he could not determine which race predominated. "I guess you would call them the world race," Martin said.

The language was predominantly Spanish but not the same Spanish he had attempted to learn in high school. He could understand very little of it, and his attempts to engage in conversation with several of the natives were unsuccessful.

As they walked along in the shopping district, Martin was very interested in the various wares on display along the sidewalks, and he could have spent the entire evening browsing around and learning more about the native culture. His companion, Scotty, had other ideas.

"I got directions to a very unusual place from old Hank. You know him. He's in the black gang, in the engine room. He's been here before. Will you come along?" Scotty asked, suddenly appearing to recognize something he had been looking for.

"What kind of a place is it?" Martin responded.

"A very unusual place. Something you have never seen or maybe never even heard of," answered Scotty. "Here is the square with a fountain and lots of pigeons in the middle. We are supposed to go down the street to the right, then about five blocks there is supposed to be a saloon with swinging doors at the top of high steps. There we are supposed to turn down a small street to the left, an alley that's hardly big enough for a car to go through."

"What's so special about this place?" Martin asked.

"Just follow me and find out. Come on!"

They followed these directions and at the end of the narrow alley they came upon several large two-story buildings which appeared to be apartments. There were many soldiers and sailors in the area of the buildings. Soldiers and sailors were going in and out the main entrances. For a minute Martin thought that this might be some group of international service organization buildings, but he soon learned differently. As they approached the main entrance door nearest them, Martin noticed that there was an Army MP and a Navy shore patrolman on duty. They were scrutinized carefully as they went through the doors.

Inside there was a long hall with many doors apparently leading into rooms. It was not like our apartment buildings at all, but more like any floor of our hotels back home. But the strange thing was that at some doors stood girls of the mixed race Martin had seen in the street. At other doors there were lines of military men and some civilians. Other doors were closed and no one stood at them.

"Just what is this, anyway?" Martin insisted.

Scotty's face widened with a sheepish grin. "This here is something we should have back in the States," he said. "Then there wouldn't be as many 'Nuts' running around the streets attacking women and all that kind of stuff. This is a legal whorehouse."

Martin was genuinely shocked. But Scotty continued, "This is controlled by the government. All of these girls are inspected regularly, so they tell me. You don't have to be scared of getting something from them. Let's look them over."

Martin had heard of things such as this, of course, but he never believed they really existed. He walked along the halls with Scotty who was examining the unoccupied girls carefully. There were all kinds and varieties; big ones, little ones, skinny ones, fat ones, tall ones, and short ones. Some were white, others black, yellow, tan or brown.

As they passed them, some of them just stood there showing as much of their wares as the rules would allow; others invited them to come in, in broken English, but using the kind of words Martin had never heard uttered from the lips of the female sex. A few walked out into the middle of the hall and urged them to come in.

"The best looking ones must be in those rooms where the guys are lined up," said Scotty. "But I never go just on looks."

"Scotty," Martin almost whispered. "I'm getting out of here. This is no place for me."

"Aw, for God's sake," said Scotty. "Look how easy this is. You may never get a chance like this again. Pick yourself one out and have yourself a good time. You'll feel like a million bucks afterwards. You probably need it as bad as I do, and this is a chance of a lifetime."

At that moment one of the girls came over to Martin, took hold of his arm and said, "Come, Saila, I gif you good. Only fi dolla."

Martin remembered the VD lectures and movies which had been shown at boot camp. Pictures of men and girls with VD sores on various parts of their bodies flashed before his eyes. He jerked his arm free and his face reddened with embarrassment and indignation. The girl was light brown, but with Latin features, she was really very pretty and pleasant. She was short and slightly plump, but not fat. Martin must have insulted her because she became angry and excited and let out a long string of words in her own tongue as she uncovered her breasts to show him that they were nice and young and firm. "Come, Saila," she said again. "Only fi dolla."

"No, thanks," Martin said with embarrassment.

She became insistent, and muttering again in her native tongue, she grabbed Martin between the legs at his crotch. He shoved her away. But just at that moment, a shore patrolman came up to them and yelled, "O. K., break it up. No rough stuff here or you get out and get out fast." He was looking at Martin.

"He ain't makin' no rough stuff," Scotty said. "That babe was twisting his arm and he didn't like her looks."

The girl ran back to her room door.

"What the hell's the difference what they look like on the top," said the S.P. "They all look alike when you turn them upside down. Now, go get yourself a jump, peacefully like a gentleman, or get the hell out of here."

"O. K., O. K.," Scotty said. "We won't give you no trouble."

The S. P. walked away. Martin was furious. That shore patrolman thought he was after the girl, getting rough with her.

"I'm getting out of here," he said, and started for the exit at the end of the hall.

"Aw, don't be like that," said Scotty. "But it's up to you. I'm going back and get that little spitfire that was after you. She looks like she could give a man his money's worth."

"I'll see you back on the ship," Martin yelled as he hurried to get out of the building.

THIRTEEN

Panama City and Unexpected Love

As soon as he left the building Martin looked for and found the alley through which they had come, and made his way back to the center square. Walking fast he wore off his astonishment and anger. "My God," he mumbled to himself. "Human beings really are animals!" But it wasn't condemnation of others only that he was expressing. For he knew that he had come perilously close to yielding to the wild, turbulent sexual desire that he knew was raging inside of him. He knew he was no better than Scotty or anyone else. He knew the lust that was in his own heart.

He was in a state of confusion and mental turmoil. Maybe Scotty was right. Scotty would come back to the ship feeling great, and he would go back feeling frustrated. Why the difference in attitudes? Is there some innate moral conscience of which some individuals are more aware than others, or is it all a matter of learning, some learning one way and others another way? He walked along the street deeply engrossed in these thoughts, thoroughly confused and undecided. He saw a church about a block down the street. He walked to it and entered. It was a Catholic church, beautifully adorned in gold and other precious metals. Its alter was a mass of golden decoration. It seemed strange to him, but it was a house of God, and he sorely needed a house of God. Up front in one of the pews was an old woman. There was no one else there. He walked about half way down the center aisle and sat down.

He sat quietly, taking in the effect of the majestic atmosphere of the church and contemplated the insignificance of man in the presence of Almighty God. There is a mighty, spiritual, creative force in the world, in the universe, he thought, which we call God and this God is beyond our understanding, even though at times a person can almost feel that he is somehow a part of this creative force. He prayed then for the strength he would need to avoid the temptations and the evil which surrounded his daily life. He prayed for the wisdom to understand the true difference between good and evil. He knew he was confused on this subject. Was everything that our religion and our culture taught us as evil, really evil? Was everything they said was good, really good? He tried to remember what Alice's letter had said about our parents misguiding us in matters of sex. Maybe they had good reasons for calling some acts evil, but are those reasons as valid now as they once had been?

While these questions were not answered, the prayer and meditation helped him get his mind back into focus again. He got up to leave feeling much better. But just as he arose and was turning to go back up the aisle, he bumped someone. It was a girl who had apparently come in while he was meditating and he hadn't noticed her. He knocked some packages out of her hand. He stooped over to pick up the packages, and just as he was about to hand them to her and excuse himself, he was captivated by her eyes. They were dark eyes, friendly and sad. He was motionless for a moment. Then realizing the awkward situation, he stammered, "I'm sorry, I didn't see you."

"Eet ees O. K., Senior," she answered and smiled, warm and friendly.

They walked down the aisle side by side, and Martin didn't know what to say for fear she wouldn't understand him. The girl kept staring at him, saying nothing. When they got outside Martin said again, "I'm sorry . . . Do you speak English?"

"Si," she answered. "But no moocho. I unerstan betta, but no speak so good."

"You must understand very good; I don't hardly understand any of your language."

"I am matramony Americana lika you."

"You are married to an American like me. You mean to a sailor?"

"Si," she answered, and a look of sadness came to her face and her eyes looked down to the white steps on which they were standing. This gave Martin a chance to see her better because she was not staring at him. Her face was beautiful and young and soft and kind, but it showed minute signs of suffering and pain; of sadness suppressed by hope and courage. She wore a sheer blouse, which accentuated her shapely bosom, and a flared skirt which was tight at the waist. She was small, almost dainty. Her skin was light brown, but soft. She looked up again into Martin's eyes and he felt the same sensation running up and down his spine that he had felt a few minutes ago when he had accidently bumped her. He knew she was trying to tell him something which she probably couldn't express in English.

"Senior ess on beeg sheep on wata?" she asked finally.

"Yes. I'm on a ship, but a small ship."

"You muss go to sheep pronto, soon?"

"I have liberty until tonight, after the sun goes down. My name is Martin Miller. What is your name?"

"Pamia Taylor."

"Do you live here in Panama City?"

"I leeve away, where no moocho adobe, no moocho streets. No in Panama Ceety, but no moocho far. You lika see I leeve?"

"Yes," he responded without a moment's hesitation, drawn by some unexplainable desire to learn more about this girl.

"Come," said the girl. She led him along the street for two blocks. At an intersection were several old beat up automobiles which served as taxi cabs. The girl climbed into the taxi. Martin followed her. The driver started down narrow streets and then out on a dirt road into the country. They traveled along at a slow, but steady pace through the countryside, occasionally passing groups of natives who looked upon them with condoning smiles. They passed here and there a small adobe building where native men sat, leaning against the walls, taking their siestas; where small native children, half naked, playing, would stare at them as they passed, some waving or shouting. Finally, they turned off into a lane which was practically grown over with grass and weeds and was lined on each side with tropical trees. At the end of the lane they came upon two mud-coated buildings. The driver pulled up in front of one of the buildings and stopped.

Pamia stepped out of the taxi and beckoned Martin to follow. The taxi pulled away. Pamia started to enter the building, but Martin momentarily hesitated, not knowing what to expect. She had said that she was married to an American. But, being driven by that desire to learn more about her, he followed.

There were two rooms. In one was an assortment of objects which indicated it was the kitchen. It had a dilapidated cook stove, rickety and crude table and chairs and a shelf with a bucket of water and various basins, pots and pans. The other room had a double bed and a dresser. It was quaint, old European furniture which might have come into this country many decades before. There was also a sort of cot, ropes strung across a wooden frame, with a scanty mattress.

The whole place could not have been called filthy, but it did not have the tidiness and the cleanliness that Martin associated with a home. But it was cooler to be there inside shielded from the hot baking sun. The girl motioned for Martin to sit on the cot, and went into the kitchen, returning in a few minutes with two tall glasses of strange smelling, strange tasting drink. He did not know what it was, but it did quench his thirst. He leaned back on a cushion propped against the wall, drank more of the drink and followed the girl's movements as she searched through the dresser drawers looking for something.

Presently she came over to him holding an old yellow-stained, large envelope. She sat down beside him on the cot, opened the envelope and emptied its contents on the cot. There were several pictures, letters and other papers.

"Sees ees my hussben," she said, showing him the pictures. One was a portrait picture of an American sailor who looked to be about Martin's own age. Martin noticed that the features of the face on the picture were somewhat like his own, and he became self-conscious looking at it. Another snapshot showed this sailor and a girl, which Martin knew immediately was the one sitting next to him, her knees touching his. It was a scene on some beach. They were in bathing suits, and Martin's eyes became fixed on the girl's image, at the bared shoulders and legs. He tore his eyes away from the picture and looked at her sitting there next to him. She smiled back at him with lips wet from the drink. Tiny, minute beads of perspiration danced in semi-circles under her eyes. Martin felt himself drawn involuntarily, instinctively toward those luscious lips. She handed him a folded paper, her expression changing suddenly again to sadness. Martin unfolded it and began to read. It was a telegram reading as follows:

WASHINGTON, D. C.
19 SEPTEMBER, 1940

MRS. PAMIA ALOSA TAYLOR

THE NAVY DEPARTMENT DEEPLY REGRETS TO IN-FORM YOU THAT YOUR HUSBAND, JOSEPH KURT TAYLOR, DIED IN THE SERVICE OF HIS COUNTRY, 16 SEPTEMBER ON BOARD HIS SHIP AT SEA. LETTER TO FOLLOW.

JON DERLINGTON, CAPTAIN, U. S. NAVY

Martin looked back into her sad eyes. There were other papers in her hand, no doubt giving all of the other details of his death. Martin quickly gathered these papers to-gether and put them back into the envelope.

"Your husband is dead. I'm sorry," he said.

"In the church," she said. "I theenk you are my hussben. That ess why I look at you so moocho."

Embarrassed at having been taken for her dead husband, at least he understood now. He took her hand into his, wanting to comfort her in her sadness. But as he did, she leaned over and put her head on his shoulder and began to cry, almost silently. Then she put her arms around his body and cried aloud, saddening sobs of loneliness and despair. Martin was overcome with compassion, sympathy and the desire to comfort her. He held her close and stroked her head. He took out his handkerchief and wiped her nose and eyes, as if she were a child. She stopped crying and lifted her face up to his. Suddenly he was overwhelmed with mixed compassion and desire. He took her head in his hands and kissed her lips and her cheeks and her eyes, and the remaining tears tasted salty on his lips.

"Pamia," he said. "You are a beautiful, sad and lonely girl." And he knew that she was a striking example of that sadness and loneliness that haunts every human heart at one time or another. Pamia clung to him desperately, as if they were in the middle of the sea drowning. Her closeness, the taste of her, and the drink were beginning to cloud Martin's mind.

"What was in the drink?" he asked, in a low, almost inaudible voice.

"Moocho fruit and rum," she answered, and mistakenly thinking that he wanted more of the drink, she went back to the kitchen and prepared two more glasses of the same.

Neither of them spoke as they consumed the refreshing drink. Then Pamia got up, went outside and returned in a moment carrying a large round metal wash tub. She placed it in the center of the kitchen floor and proceeded to fill it with water, carrying it by the bucket from somewhere outside.   Martin sat there, perspiring profusely, and watched her, fascinated and curious. When the tub was full of water, Pamia began to remove her clothing. First she took off her shoes and anklets, then her blouse and skirt. When she stood there beside the tub clad only in her sheer panties, Martin starred with incredibility, not knowing what to do or what to say. The drink was clouding his mind.

Pamia, however, proceeded without shame or misgivings to remove her panties. When she stood there before him completely naked, Martin was in a state of intense conflict and confusion.

She was beautiful--simply, radiantly beautiful. If only he could talk her language, he thought, he would try to explain to her that this sort of thing should not be done by a girl so beautiful, so wonderful as she. He would explain to her that all of the religious and moral laws, the niceties which he had been taught prohibited such behavior as she was now displaying. But in the next flash of thought he wondered why he should think there was anything wrong with what she was doing. She was so utterly unpretentious, so unaffected, so innocently natural.

"Come," she said. "The bath ees good. My hussben teech me, the bath ees good."

Martin's eyes fixed upon her luscious body again. He arose as if in a trance and removed his clothing with furious speed. They bathed together, standing in the cool refreshing water, soaping each other and pouring cooking pots full of water over one another, simulating a shower. And as he washed away the perspiration and dust from his body, Martin also seemed to be washing away all of the guilt and the shame associated with sex which had been ingrained in his mind from childhood.

When they stepped out of the tub, and dried off, Martin put his arm around Pamia's naked waist, and led her boldly to the bedroom. They lay down together on the bed, and while he looked at Pamia's beautiful body, he thought of Alice and Angela, and all three of their images blended into that one ideal woman which he many times had seen in his dreams. Desire sprang forth from the depths of his physical and mental being and Martin wanted to lavish upon that one woman all the love that cried out with every heartbeat for fulfillment. But the convictions of his childhood training, his religious training, the inhibitions ingrained during his formative years, momentarily emerged. "Oh, merciful God," he cried out aloud. "Have your prophets and priests interpreted your will correctly? How can this be sin?"

Pamia, who did not understand all of the words, but sensing Martin's apparent conflict, placed her hands upon him gently, stroked his body tenderly, and caressed him as if he were a child, as she muttered soothing words of love. Then, slowly, the conflict was resolved. His body began to relax and he commenced making love to Pamia naturally, manly, tenderly and without restraint. They caressed one another unselfishly, manipulating, fondling, kissing without haste and with all the variety known to uninhabited human beings; and at the climax all the anguish and the conflict had vanished. Relaxed now, relieved and at peace with the universe, they lay side by side and drifted into peaceful, dreamless sleep.

FOURTEEN

Before the Captain's Mast

Hours later Martin woke up in the quiet darkness of early morning. He felt wonderfully happy, peaceful and contented. Pamia's soft, delicate, perspired body lay cuddled in his arms. She was sleeping soundly. He drew her closer, sank his head deeper into the pillow and was about to go back to sleep, when suddenly he awoke to reality. He realized he was in trouble. He sat up in a flash, shaking Pamia nervously.

"Pamia, Pamia," he called out. "Wake up, Pamia, I am late. I am AOL. I may miss the ship."

The girl, confused and only half awake, fumbled in the darkness to light the candle on the little table beside the bed. "I'm sorry, I'm so sorry," she said, after the candle was burning.

"It's not your fault," said Martin. "My clothes, my clothes. Where are they? Quick!"

She handed them to him and he dressed hurriedly.

"How will I get back to the ship?" he asked. "It is very dark outside and I do not know the way."

"Maybe we must walk," said Pamia. "I will show the way. Maybe the bus will come."

They left the house and hurried back down the lane in the darkness, holding hands, almost running. When they reached the main road it was just as dark as in the lane. Off in the distance they could see the lights of Panama

City. They continued walking swiftly, still holding hands. On foot, it seemed like an endless road ahead of them. After about fifteen minutes of this, Martin could hear Pamia panting. He slowed the pace.

"You had better go back to your house," he said. "I'll find the way back to the ship."

"No, no!" cried Pamia. "You cannot find the way. Do not stop. You will be in great trouble." She pulled his arm, leading the way.

Half an hour later, hurrying along the road, but not as fast anymore, they heard the low hum of an engine behind them. It grew steadily louder. Pamia stopped and said, "The bus, it is the bus."

"Thank God!" exclaimed Martin, relieved, as the beams of the headlights from the bus crawled upon them.

But when momentarily the lights rested on Pamia's form and lit her up like the statue of a Goddess of old, and Martin could see her, bare-footed and covered only with the thin blouse and skirt, for a brief moment he wished he were not going back to the ship. He wished he could forget all about Navy life, forget all of the past, and stay there with her forever.

But in a few moments the bus was only a few feet away from them and they flagged it down. Martin quickly picked up Pamia and held her with a deep, breathless kiss.

"From here I must go alone, but I will be back."

"When will you come?" she asked.

"I don't know when I'll have liberty again, but I'll be back," he answered. "You wait for me."

"You will no come back. You must give me money now."

"Money?" Martin asked, looking at her in disbelief.

"Si," she said. "Moocho money. Americana always give money. Americana very rich."

In haste and confusion, Martin pulled the roll of American dollar bills from his jumper pocket, pulled off three dollars for himself and pressed the rest of it into Pamia's dainty hand.

The bus, which looked like an American milk delivery truck, squeaked to a stop alongside of them, and as he climbed aboard, Martin squeezed Pamia's hand firmly. "I guess this is good-bye," he said.

"Bye, bye," she said sadly.

The sleepy driver started the bus with a jerk, and Martin leaned out of the door to wave. Pamia waved back at him, and then disappeared into the darkness.

When the bus dropped him off at the Naval Base gate, he gave the driver the remaining three dollars, and then ran down the dock to the ship. His heart raced madly as he climbed up the gang-plank.

"Who goes there?" yelled the O. D., as Martin stepped over the side of the ship.

"Martin Miller, Sir, returning from liberty," he answered.

"Don't you know that liberty was up at 2400 hours last night?"

"Yes, Sir," he answered.

"Then you know I'll have to put you on report for being AOL," said the officer.

"Martin's heart sank. "Yes, Sir," he repeated, hanging his head. This would mean that he would have to go to Captain's Mast, and he had heard of some of the severe punishments which had been handed out by their Captain. He hurried down to the crew's quarters, changed into dungarees and then rushed back up to the mess hall where he joined Scotty. Scotty had a favorite corner in the mess hall where he spent most of his off duty hours, often reading.

"What happened to you?" he asked with obvious and intense curiosity.

"You probably wouldn't believe it if I told you," Martin answered.

"You wouldn't believe what I did after you ran off from that legal whorehouse either," Scotty said.

"Well, I don't think I want to know what you did, but I did have a very unusual experience and I'd appreciate your opinion about it."

"Sure, sure," Scotty said, again with obvious curiosity.

Martin told him the gist of the story, leaving out some of the more intimate details.

"Well," Scotty said, smiling broadly. "It sounds to me like you got picked up by a streetwalker working on her own, and them's the worst kind as far as I'm concerned."

"Oh, I can't believe that!" Martin said, emphatically. "I told you I met her in a church."

"She probably saw you go in and followed you. You probably looked like a good mark for her."

"You really think that's true?" Martin asked, chagrinned.

"Looks like it to me," Scotty said, laughing.

"Good God Almighty Damn! I'll never believe that," Martin almost shouted, as he left the mess hall to report for duty on the bridge.

The Captain had gone ashore to receive future sailing orders, and this meant that there would be no shore leave for the rest of the officers and men until he returned.

There was much grumbling and complaining by the crew as they watched liberty parties coming and going on other ships.

But it made no difference to Martin. He had been placed on report, and he was now considered a prisoner-at-large. He would not be granted any further liberty until after he had faced Captain's Mast.

This dreaded ordeal came much sooner than expected, for when the Captain returned aboard ship he announced that they would remain in the port of Balboa for a period of one week. Captain's Mast was scheduled for the third day in port. It was to be held on the bridge. All offenders who had been placed on report since the date of the last Captain's Mast were instructed to appear there in dress white uniform.

When Martin got to the bridge he was instructed to step into line along with six other enlisted men. It seemed like an endless wait to Martin while preparations were being made for this minor military court. The preparations seemed too elaborate, almost as if they were preparing for a full military court-martial. Several officers, also in full dress whites, were on the bridge, looking stern-faced and solemn. The Captain's conning chair, normally used by the officer of the deck for full observation and control of the ship while underway, served as a judge's bench. Alongside of it stood the ship's yeoman holding the offenders' personnel records, also looking stern-faced and dignified. Then, finally, the O. D. shouting through the brass speaker tube, formally announced: "All preparations are completed for Captain's Mast, Captain."

"Very well," the Captain responded.

Another long wait, then the Captain appeared on the bridge, wearing a spotless white full dress uniform.

"Attention on deck!" the Master-at-Arms yelled, and instantly every officer and man became as rigid as a telegraph pole.

The Captain stepped up to his makeshift judge's bench.

"The Captain's Mast is now in session. All hands salute," the Master-at-Arms said. Everyone saluted the Captain.

"Very well," he said, calmly and assertively, after returning the salute. "First case."

"Robert Uhallar, Seaman Second Class," called out the yeoman, handing the offender's record to the Captain.

Uhallar stepped up before the Captain, saluted, then removed his white hat, as he had been instructed. He stood rigidly at attention while the Captain read the charges against him.

"You are charged with drunk and disorderly conduct while on authorized liberty in Panama City, Republic of Panama," said the Captain. "What do you have to say for yourself?"

"Nothing, Sir," said Uhallar timidly.

"Nothing," said the Captain, in a tone which started low and ended high. "You were so disorderly and so drunk that the civil authorities had to take you into custody and turn you over to the shore patrol, and you have nothing to say?"

"It was my birthday, Sir," Uhallar responded.

"Well, birthday, or no birthday," said the Captain. "When you are wearing the uniform of the United States Navy, you are to conduct yourself properly, like a good

Navy man. If you can't handle your liquor, then don't drink it." He paged through the man's record.

"I see this is your second offense for drunkenness. Were you celebrating your birthday the first time too?"

"No, Sir," the offender answered.

"Well, since it was your birthday, I'm going to overlook it this time. But I'm going to put a warning slip in your record, which will stay in for six months. So, don't let me see you up here again. If I do, I'll put you in the brig for the maximum time. Do you understand that?"

"Yes, Sir. Aye, aye, Sir," said Uhallar with uncontrolled appreciation in his voice. He replaced his white hat on his head, saluted and then walked off the bridge.

"Next case," said the Captain, handing the seaman's record to the yeoman. He made an effort to conceal the smile on his face.

Standing there in line on the wing of the bridge only a few feet from the Captain, Martin listened intently to the proceedings of the first case. The charge had sounded very serious as he heard the Captain read it off and his stomach muscles tightened and his heart pounded faster, and he felt a certain sympathy for the accused man standing there. But when he heard the verdict, he was astonished. He had heard that the Captain's punishments were always harsh for the offense involved. But now he had taken into account that it was the man's birthday, in spite of the severity of the offense. Martin gained a new respect for the Captain's judgement.

"Herbert Doggert, Signalman First Class," called out the yeoman. "Stand before the Captain."

The signalman stepped forward, saluted, and removed his white hat.

The Captain read the charge to himself. He looked up, first at the other officers and men rimming the bridge with disbelief on his face. Then he looked scornfully into the face of the accused. "You are charged with urinating on the base of a statue while on authorized liberty in the port of Balboa, Republic of Panama," said the Captain, in a scornful, half whisper. "What have YOU to say about that?"

"I'm sorry, Sir."

"You're sorry!" the Captain roared. "You're sorry is right. You're a sorry sight, a despicable, disgusting sight. You are the worst kind of scoundrel in this man's Navy. You are a regular Navy man, and in view of the fact that your case does not deserve any further consideration, I am going to confine you to the brig aboard this ship for a period of ten days on bread and water, with a full ration every third day. And, if you ever come before me again for anything that brings such disgrace on the United States Navy, I'm going to recommend you for a General Court Martial and hope they give you a bad conduct discharge. Is that CLEAR?"

The offender did not answer.

"IS THAT UNDERSTOOD?"

"Aye, aye, Sir," Doggert quickly said.

"Next case," the Captain said, dismissing Doggert without the usual formalities, shaking with anger, as he thrust the offender's record into the yeoman's hand with such force it caused him to drop the other records. There was a delay and a shuffling of papers and records while the yeoman gathered them up and tried to put them back into order.

"Martin Miller, Seaman Second Class," sounded the yeoman's voice, loud and clear.

Martin stepped before the Captain without a moment's hesitation. He gave a snappy salute and removed his white hat. He looked directly at the Captain, who was looking down at his record. He shifted his eyes to the faces of the other officers and men on the bridge, and he truly felt like the accused. Within him was the universal emotion of every man who has ever stood accused and awaiting judgement, however minor, or severe the offense; ready to absolve himself of guilt on the basis of the "circumstances" which caused him to disobey the rules.

The Captain raised his eyes and directed them squarely into Martin's. He suddenly felt as if every detail of his affair with Pamia on that night on which he had come back to his ship AOL had been laid bare by those eyes. He assumed that the mind behind those eyes would evaluate the circumstances as he himself had. The circumstances justified his being AOL, he reasoned.

"You are charged with being absent over leave for a period of seven hours, having failed to return to your ship at the expiration of authorized liberty while in the port of Balboa, Republic of Panama. What do you have to say about that?"

"Well, Sir, I ah, I was in a church, Sir, and I met this local girl in the church, and . . ."

"A girl. I see," the Captain interrupted, a smile breaking slightly at the corners of his lips, which he immediately wiped off. "Well, I want to tell you something, son. Girls have been the cause of more bad conduct and dishonorable discharges from the Navy than any other thing I know of. That is a fact of life which every Navy man must adjust himself to. You cannot let your love affairs interfere with your duty in the Navy. Do you realize that you might have missed your ship if we had set sail early this morning, and that is one of the most serious offenses you can commit?"

"Yes, Sir," Martin answered. "But you don't understand, Sir. This was not just . . ."

"I DON'T UNDERSTAND?" the Captain roared. "Now you see here, young man!" He paused, and it was apparent that he was struggling hard not to lose his temper. He took a deep breath and continued in a subdued, fatherly-like manner: "I have been in this man's Navy a good many years. I am the Captain of this ship, and I understand a lot more than you seem to think. I have read over your record, as I have read every other man's record on this ship. You haven't been on active duty very long, but so far your record has been a good one. But I'm going to warn you right now--you have come very close to committing contempt of the Commanding Officer of this ship, an even more serious offense than the one you are now on report for. Because of your record, I'm going to overlook it this time. But as a reminder for you to always get back on board your ship on time, regardless of circumstances, you are restricted to this ship for the remainder of our stay in the Panama area. Do you think that will be enough of a reminder of what I have said?"

"Yes, Sir. Yes, Sir. Aye, aye, Sir," Martin said, thoroughly impressed.

"Very well, you are dismissed."

He hurried off of the bridge as they were calling the next offender. He hadn't anticipated the Captain's response to his attempt to defend himself, and he was seriously shaken. He realized how close he had come to a further breach of Navy rules and regulations. But at the same time he was relieved that his punishment had not been more than restriction to the ship. He wondered if that would go into his record.

Coming down off the bridge he passed Lieutenant Rosetto, who was on his way to the wardroom.

"Good morning, Sir," Martin said.

"G'morning, Martin," answered Rosetto. "How'd you do at Captain's Mast? I saw you were on report for being AOL."

"The Captain restricted me to the ship while we're in Panama, Sir," he answered. He tried to avoid Rosetto's eyes. He felt deluged by self-consciousness and guilt, and he hoped Rosetto had not heard that there was a girl involved. It was stupid of me to mention that at Captain's Mast, he thought.

"You were lucky. But since it was your first offense-- that probably worked in your favor. I heard you got lost in Panama City. Better not travel alone in strange cities, at least until you know your way around better."

"Thanks, Lieutenant, I'll remember that," Martin sighed.

FIFTEEN

Shocking News

Because he was restricted to the ship, two weeks seemed like a long time to Martin. He envied the daily liberty parties he saw coming and going. He worked his monotonous job of scraping blistered paint and repainting steel decks and bulkheads, and he stood his watches on the bridge. It was during these watches on the bridge that Lieutenant Rosetto would casually step out of the chart room and engage Martin in conversation. It would start out usually on the subject of navigation, plotting a course, etc., and then cover a wide range of subjects and invariably wind up with religion.

"Although we are from different religions, we apparently have similar types of doubts about our religions," Rosetto said one night. But my parents are such strict Catholics that I just couldn't discuss any doubts I had with them. There's no questioning the dogma or the authority of the Catholic Church, as far as my parents are concerned. So, I forgot about religion and avoided it as much as possible, especially after I left home to go to the Naval Academy. But I have a little book which discusses religion and human spirituality from a completely different and daring point of view. I've gotten some good ideas from it and my guess is that you would benefit from it too. If you're interested remind me some time when we're off duty. I'll dig it out and loan it to you--if your interested."

"Yes, Lieutenant," Martin answered, "I'm very much interested, I'll remind you. Thank you."

But finally the time was up. A huge concrete barge which they had been waiting for while it was being unloaded was now ready and preparations were made to leave Balboa and Panama Bay. It was a happy day for Martin. It meant the end of his confinement to the ship. He had served his time, so to speak, for having broken the Navy rules and regulations. But in a way it was also a sad day. On the one hand he would be getting away from the area which had caused him so much trouble and embarrassment; but on the other hand, he could not escape the longing desire to see Pamia again, to hold her dainty body in his arms again, to have her swear that what Scotty said about her was false. But, of course, at this point, that was impossible.

Perhaps it is for the best, he thought, for any more contact with Pamia would most likely only cause further embarrassment. It is probably better this way. Besides, he also was unable to shake off the feelings of guilt which stemmed from this relationship with Pamia whenever he thought of his relationship with Angela. He had entered into a serious commitment with Angela and reason told him that it was wrong to have had the affair with Pamia. Events such as this are hard to understand, he thought. He hadn't planned anything like that. It just happened that way. But it seems that it shouldn't have happened. He would have to forget it. "Chalk it up to experience," his father would have said, "and let it be a lesson to you."

Early the next morning they cast off from the pier to which they had been tied and maneuvered into a clear area in Panama Bay.

"We gotta heave-to here until those little harbor tugs bring that big barge into position for us to take it in tow," Chief McCroye said. The barge was a huge floating warehouse used for Naval supplies. It was one of the many hundreds of auxiliary vessels that are an integral part of Navy logistics.

"What do you mean 'we gotta heave-to, Chief?" asked Martin.

"Well you know, they cut the power on the prop, and we maintain our position, without anchoring. If we drift out of position, then they rev up the engines and bring it back. Know what I mean.?"

"Yeah, I know what you mean now. I've watched other ships doing it." answered Martin.

When the barge was in position, Scotty and Martin worked with the deck gang in the operation of making fast the huge steel cable which was the fleet tug's main towing line. This was done by first shooting a small line over to the line-handling men on the barge, using a gun similar in shape and size to a shotgun.

"Get it right over the bow of that barge," Chief Mc-Croye commanded. Martin fired and hit the target. To the end of this was attached a series of increasingly heavier manila lines which the barge men pulled aboard the barge. Then to the last of these was attached the main steel towing cable. As it was paid out from the fleet tug's powerful main electric winch, it too was hauled aboard the barge by means of the barge's winch and made fast.

As these preparations were being made, the Navy mail boat came up alongside to make a last minute delivery of mail. With this accomplished and the barge in tow, the Chief Boatswain notified the bridge and in minutes Martin could feel the powerful main propeller come to life. The USS FLEET TUG moved slowly at first, churning the water behind it furiously, beating it into a chaotic, milky, foamy substance. But gradually they picked up speed, and it was amazing to see that gigantic concrete vessel moving in unison with the fleet tug. The main tow line cable hung in a large arch and dipped deeply into the water, while the barge appeared to be moving along under its own power, many ship lengths behind the ship.

They steamed out of the bay with the barge following steadily behind. They passed Perlas Island, and at a steady forward speed, through the Gulf of Panama. Then, at last, they moved out into the open waters of the Pacific Ocean.

Even though they were only on the fringe of it, Martin could already feel the vastness and the strange force of this immeasurable body of water. They were fortunate to have steamed into the Pacific Ocean on this particular day. For, although it is known that the Pacific is not always like this, on this particular day, the weather was as clear as it is possible to be. The sea was as calm and tranquil as a small lake on a windless day. Looking out as far as he could see to the horizon, the ocean appeared to be one endless glass mirror. Looking in every direction, he could not see the slightest ripple on those endless miles of blue tranquil water. Martin imagined that this is how it must have looked when its discoverer, Balboa, first fixed his gaze upon it those hundreds of years ago. He was thrilled by the thought that he was here in the vicinity of the spot where that great explorer once had been.

For the next two weeks they cruised at a slow but steady pace, northward, along the coasts of Costa Rica, Nicaragua, Salvador, Guatemala and Mexico. Many times they came into sight of the shoreline on the starboard side, but always to port they could see nothing but the vast blue waters of the Pacific.

Soon after they were underway, steering their steady course, the Boatswain piped down mail call. Martin felt himself shaking with excitement as he reached for his letters from the Boatswain who was handing out the mail to the deck gang. There were three letters for him, one from his mother, one from Cathy Welsh, and to his surprise, one, with the familiar perfumed odor, from Alice Schneider.

He was extremely curious about Alice's letter, but first he opened his mother's. It was her usual inquiry into his health. Plus she had heard about Alice's marriage from Margaret, and she gave her usual comment that she thought it was for the best that things had worked out as they had. "What is meant to be, is meant to be," she reminded him, and she repeated her plea that he quit the Navy as soon as possible and become a minister which is the only life she knew that would be right for him. But this also reminded him that his mother was a lot more domineering than he had realized when he was under her wing. She was persistent and she often ended up getting her way in family matters, whether or not it was best for some one else or not. But, that's the way she was, he thought, and no one was likely to change her. The thought flashed through his mind for a split second that maybe that's why he "ran off to the Navy." He could see clearly now that his father, often unable to dissuade her from some unacceptable idea or goal, had just wound up avoiding her. And, looking back, he could see now that's why they always seemed to be running on separate tracks. It occurred to him that his mother had been a much greater influence in his life than he previously recognized. Would he have ever thought of becoming a minister without her incessant maneuvering? He wasn't sure now.

But he was anxious to read his other letters. He was particularly anxious to learn why Cathy Welsh would be writing to him. He opened her letter next. She thought of him when she attended Jim Johnson's funeral back home in Winston-Salem. Johnson's folks and her folks had been friends and neighbors for many years, and since she had been dating Jim, they thought it only right that she should go with them to Jim's funeral. She was glad she went because she felt awful when she read in the paper about his death in a street fight on the same night that she had broken off with him and had Martin and her father throw him out of the house. She felt guilty about it and wondered if what she did made him get so drunk that night and maybe aggravated his condition.

The reason she was writing to Martin, she wrote, is that she had heard that there was another one of his shipmates in the fight and she wondered if Martin knew anything about it. She had told Johnson's parents after the funeral that she would find out all she could for them. They were not satisfied with the Navy's report of his death. She would appreciate hearing from him if he heard anything about it aboard ship, and if ever he came back to Norfolk he should get in touch with her. Her letter exuded sincerity, and he was happy that she remembered him and made the effort to write to him. Nevertheless, there were some disturbing comments in her letter also that he would get back to later.

He could hold off no longer. It was Alice's letter he wanted to read, and he ripped it open as his heart raced furiously. He read as follows:

September 25, 1941

Dear Martin,

I thought my last letter was difficult to write, and it was, but this one is even more difficult. Charles and I were married on September 17th, a week after I wrote you that last letter. Then yesterday I went to see a doctor, a gynecologist, because I was having some unusual problems. I just don't know how to say this, Martin, I have always had irregular menstrual periods. To begin with I didn't start menstruating as early as some of the other girls I know, but it was never really a problem and I never had to worry--you know that! And because my period was always irregular, I never paid much attention to it. If I had it, I had it, and if I didn't, I didn't.

Well, by now you have no doubt guessed it, the doctor told me, yesterday, that I am four months pregnant. I know this sounds absurd, ridiculous and unbelievable, I just can hardly believe it myself. But, of course I have to believe it. The doctor is 100% sure. I don't know what to do. I haven't even told Charles as yet. It just doesn't seem possible, because I didn't have any real indication of being pregnant until just last week when I noticed I was gaining weight and beginning to show. Only then did I stop to think about when I had had my last period, and even though I did have some blood spots about a month ago, I realize I should have known. But honestly and truly, Martin, I was just simply not consciously aware that I was pregnant.

According to the doctor, I got pregnant in early June, which, of course, is the time we made love in the car, up on the mountain. I know that you will recognize that only you could be the father.

Oh, my God, Martin, what am I going to do? I have certainly made a mess of things. What good has all this education done for me? I can't believe that I have been so stupid. There I was, blaming my parents for misleading me, when at the same time they were spending their hard earned money to give me an education, and look what I have done with it! What will every one think of me? What will my parents think of me? What will Charles think of me? What must you think of me? I have betrayed you in the worst possible way, and now Charles too is betrayed.

There is no way I can hide the fact that I'm pregnant and there is no question that you made me pregnant. I have to tell Charles tonight, and then God only knows where I'll stand. I suppose at this point we could get an annulment. Charles is a Catholic and I had agreed to raise our children Catholic, but, for Heaven's sake, what has that to do with it?

Martin, is there any way you can possibly forgive me? I mean can you forgive me for not waiting, for marrying Charles? I know I betrayed you. I acted too hastily, too emotionally, too immaturely. But, I am not in this mess alone. You also acted impulsively and immaturely when you made me submit, and for that I'll have to forgive you. . . when I think of it . . . why did you do it without a rubber?. Any blundering high school kid knows better than that. Oh, I know, love, passion, impulse--and I left you do it! It's too late to think about that now. I know your ship has sailed for far away places, and this letter may not reach you any time soon. But please, Martin, write me as soon as you *possibly can. I need your help now more than ever, but I know now, I've always needed you. I'll always love you.*

Sincerely,

Alice.

"Good God," Martin said under his breath, as he finished her letter. I got her pregnant, he thought, that's for sure! She's in one heck of a predicament, and there's nothing I can do about it now, he thought. I'll call her from the next port. A baby. I'm going to be the father of a baby. Good God! What a development. I'll have to take time to think about this. This changes everything.

The slow, steady pace northward continued and when they finally came into close proximity of the shores of California, the Executive Officer announced that their next port of call was San Francisco.

"Man, San Francisco! That's one of the best damn liberty ports in the world," an old-timer said to Martin. And he shared the excitement and enthusiasm over the prospects of being able to go ashore in that famous city. At the speed they were traveling, however, it would be two more monotonous days of the steady roar of the ship's twin-diesel engines and the rumble of the gigantic main propulsion electric motor, turning its bull-like propeller, as the sturdy Navy craft plowed through the Pacific ocean's submissive blue waters, before they would disembark in the shadow of the Golden Gate.

SIXTEEN

A Revolting Development

On the third morning after the Executive Officer's announcement, that San Francisco would be their next port-of-call, as Martin came up from below decks, they were steaming into the San Francisco Bay, and he saw for the first time that spectacular sight, the Golden Gate Bridge. He had often heard about this famous bridge, but it had always seemed so far away. Now he stood in awe as he looked up at the great span with his own eyes.

But in a short time they had passed under the bridge and were in sight of that desolate looking mass of rock and concrete called Alcatraz Island. A seaman leaning on the ship's rail alongside of Martin said aloud and to no one in particular, "Don't feel bad fellows, our ship is almost as bad as your prison island." Martin was not sure he understood what the similarity was, but the gray mass fascinated him, and he continued to look at it even when they had passed it and it was disappearing into the distance behind them. Alcatraz, he thought, what was it he had heard it called? A warehouse for the country's worst criminals: killers, rapists, and human animals. What was the difference between those poor creatures and their fellow man? Some small, minute brain matter, something physical, perhaps. Or was it purely mental, spiritual, the absence of an innate moral conscience, maybe. Our human nature is surely a strange mixture of animal instinct, but laced with some spiritual or divine essence. Is human nature really the same in all individual human beings, or are there some human attributes which not every human being possesses? Are these attributes passed on from one generation to the next by the genes, arbitrarily, like the other human characteristics, and by this means making some individuals more or less animal, more or less human, more or less intelligent than others? Is is possible that some human beings had intelligent progenitors and others didn't, and those killers and rapists there on Alcatraz simply didn't get the right combination of genes when they were conceived? He thought of Jim Johnson's death, and he realized that there was only a very thin line separating his own situation from those miserable imprisoned creatures of Alcatraz.

This mediation had taken him far from an awareness of his surroundings and he hadn't noticed that they were approaching the docks of the San Francisco waterfront.

"Hey, Miller, wake up and lend a hand there with the bow lines," the deck officer yelled.

"Aye, aye, Sir." Martin quickly responded as his attention was abruptly drawn to the pier to which they were now in the process of mooring. It was a small commercial pier, adjacent to Fisherman's Wharf. Curious passersby stopped to look over the powerful little Navy craft. Nearby he could see the San Francisco cable cars running up the center of a street headed up the hill toward center city. He had heard so much about this city and its cable cars that he was anxious to go ashore and see it for himself.

Again, no shore liberty was granted until the Captain would return with new sailing orders. However, a mail party was dispatched immediately in order to get their mail as fast as possible from the Fleet Postmaster.

That night after the evening meal Martin and Scotty shared a local newspaper which they bought from a vendor who had been allowed aboard. Martin noted the date, November 9, 1941. It was almost as if he had lost touch with the world since they left New York almost a month ago. He had not paid any attention to news of the world since that time. The front-page news was still all about Hitler's war in Europe. By this time the Germans had overrun most of Europe and the Balkans. They were driving wedges through Russia, and were now on the doorstep of Moscow. Only England had not been occupied, even though it had been pounded ruthlessly by the German Luftwaffe. He wondered again why his ship had been transferred to the Pacific fleet when there seemed to be such an urgent need for ships in the Atlantic. Although there was an article on one of the inside pages of the newspaper indicating that the U. S. Ambassador to Japan was getting signs that the Japanese might be planning some type of diplomatic initiative to pressure the U. S. into some type of an agreement favoring Japan. Sentiment in the U. S. was to stay out of the war even though the USS KEARNEY, a Navy destroyer had been hit off the coast of Iceland, and the USS REUBEN JAMES, also a destroyer, was sunk by a German U-Boat while on convoy duty off of Iceland, with a loss of 96 American lives. The world is in a turmoil, it is being turned upside-down by the Germans, Martin thought. How long can the U. S. stay out of it?

Martin passed the news section to Scotty and leaned against the bulkhead to reflect on these serious matters, when the mail party returned with the mail. It was an unusually large amount which had accumulated since their last mail in Panama. Martin had a larger stack of letters than he had ever received before. There was one from his mother, one from Margaret, several from Angela, one from his brother, Fred, and, he was surprised to see, another one from Alice.

He hadn't written in response to Alice's shocking letter about being pregnant. He had decided to call her as soon as he could get ashore. But he still didn't know what he would tell her. There was no question that he was the father of the baby she was carrying. But, she was married! She had broken their engagement, turned him down and married another man. How could she have been so stupid as not to know that she was pregnant when she married him? Why did she do it? How could he forgive her for treating him that way just because he joined the Navy to serve for one year. But, damn it, he loved Alice. He had never wanted anyone else for a wife. She would just have to get a divorce and go home and wait for him to finish serving his year in the Navy, he thought. What else could they do. Maybe things would never be the same as they once had been, but there didn't seem to be any other choice. But, what about Angela? Good God, he had made a definite commitment to Angela. He had an obligation to Angela now, and it was Alice's fault, he thought. He never would have gotten involved with Angela if Alice hadn't broken the engagement and married some one else. Damn it! What did she expect him to do? But, of course, she didn't know about Angela.

Now, here was another letter from Alice. He ripped it open and hurriedly read it. It was a long letter. It was factual, informative and unemotional. She told Charles how she had gone to the doctor and found she was pregnant at least three months before they were married, and that Martin was the father, she wrote.

At first Charles was furious. But he is a very gentle and educated man, and they reasoned together that it wouldn't benefit anyone if they would get a divorce. He suggested that they not mention the fact that he wasn't the father and raise the child as their own. No one would ever have to know. After all, they were married! But Charles was really upset when he learned she had already told Martin. But he still suggested maybe Martin wouldn't mind if he wouldn't have to support the child. Besides, Charles loves her and doesn't want to give her up for any reason. Everything else was going so well for them; she was working on her masters and Charles was teaching and they had this beautiful apartment. In a way she was sad that things had turned out this way. "But, we're all adults now," she wrote, "and we have to be practical. There are so many choices in life and we are free to choose whatever is best for us. We must make life whatever we want it to be. You chose joining the Navy as a means to finding direction and meaning in your life, and I chose to marry Charles, and we all have to live with our choices. Charles says we are free to choose whatever we want in life, but we must also be responsible for our choices, we can't blame our choices on circumstances or fate or God. I knows this flies in the face of our Judeo-Christian heritage, but I'm learning that there is much more to life than what we learned in Sunday school."

She ended her letter with, "Since I don't know where you are, and you have made your commitment to the Navy, perhaps it is best if Charles raises the child as his own. This will be best for everyone concerned. It will save us all embarrassment. I hope you find this agreeable."

Jesus! What is that girl trying to do to me? I never get a chance to give an opinion or make a comment before she makes a decision and goes ahead and does what she damn well pleases. Where is my choice in all this? he thought. First she asks for my help and then immediately proceeds as if I don't exist. Then she tells me about it afterwards. By God, he thought, this does it. I would have called her and told her to get a divorce, go home and have the baby and we could get married at the first opportunity. Damn, she infuriates me! Martin went out on the main deck to get some fresh air and had just returned and seated himself at one of the tables in the mess hall to read his other letters when Scotty came over and sat down alongside him. His face bore a very serious and troubled expression. It was an expression that Martin had never seen on him before, and he knew immediately that there must be something very unusual troubling him.

"What's up?" Martin asked, after waiting a long time for Scotty to say something.

"Well, I, ah, got this letter from, ah . . . I guess you better read it."

Martin took the letter from Scotty. The handwriting was familiar. It was Margaret's. He read as follows:

New York, N. Y.
November 3, 1941

Dearest Scotty,
*   You have never written to me and you haven't answered either of the two letters which I sent to you. I hope that is only be-*

cause of a delay in the Navy mail, which I suppose is possible since I don't know where you are. That makes my writing this letter so much harder, but there is simply no other way for me to tell you. I missed my last two periods--which means I'm pregnant.

Oh, Scotty, I am scared to death, not knowing where you are or when and if I'll ever see you again. You told me you loved me, and Oh God, I hope you meant it, Scotty, because I really do love you.

I have an appointment with the doctor next week. Please get in touch with me as soon as you can.

All my love,

Margaret.

Martin was stupefied. He thrust the letter back into Scotty's hand and looked at him in disbelief. They sat staring at one another for a long time, trying to read each other's thoughts. Through Martin's mind ran mixed pictures of the scene at Margaret's apartment which had embarrassed him and of Scotty in that house of prostitution in Panama City; he saw too, himself and Pamia in her little home. He had feelings of approval and of disapproval, of good, bad and indifference all rolled up into one confusing thought. He tried to shake off these feelings and shut out the pictures from his mind. He wanted to think straight, but he couldn't contain it, he completely lost control.

"What the hell are you going to do?" he finally asked angrily.

"What would you do?" Scotty returned.

"Well, hell, there isn't any choice as far as I'm concerned. There's only one thing you can do, get to Margaret as fast as you can. I had no idea Margaret was that much in love with you. But, you so and so, how could you do what you did in Panama when you knew about you and Margaret--for all I know you probably have the claps, or worse. One of the guys in the deck gang got the VD and he was at the same place." Martin could control himself no longer. He got up from the table, grabbed Scotty by the front of his T-shirt and lashed out at him with a right fist to the side of Scotty's head. Scotty pulled loose and backed away.

"Take it easy, Mart, take it easy. Look, I knew that's the first thing you'd think of, and I want to tell you about that. Honest to God, Martin, I didn't want to admit it, but after you left that cathouse I went into the room with that spitfire that was after you, but I didn't do anything, honest to God, not a thing. I know it might be hard for you to believe, but I no sooner got into the room with her and looked around that crummy place when I started to think about Margaret and what a good, clean, wonderful girl she is. I realized then that I really fell for her, that we fell hard the minute we met. So I left the place a couple of minutes after you. I thought maybe I could catch up with you, but I didn't see you around no more, so I went into one of them little joints, and I drank that filthy rum until I was stiff and blind. I didn't want to see nothin' or feel nothin' or think about nothin' no more. I was lucky a couple of the guys from the ship found me and carried me back to the ship, or I might still be there. Believe me, Mart, there ain't a day or night gone by since I met your sister that I haven't tried to get her out of my mind. I figured that going to that cat house would cure me of the idea that I was in love with Margaret, but . . ."

"Why didn't you want to be in love with her?"

"I don't know exactly. I guess it's because I was in love once before and I know how it gets you all tied down and I didn't want to get tied down. But, I guess I've really got it bad this time. I really do want to marry her--especially now."

Martin thought of his experience with Pamia. He knew how suddenly, how forcefully a man or a woman can become overpowered by love, or sex, or passion, infatuation or desire, or whatever it is that takes place between a man and a woman. He remembered his experience with Angela and he could sympathize with and appreciate the torment that Scotty was going through.

"So what are you going to do?"

"Well, I guess I'll try to get emergency leave and head for New York. Will you go with me to see the Exec.? I guess I'll have to tell him the real reason I want the emergency leave, and I'll need you to back me up."

"O. K., Scotty. Look, I'm sorry I flew off the handle. I just got another letter from Alice that has my head spinning, but I'll tell you about it some other time. Let's go see the Exec."

"O. K., good," Scotty said and he extended his hand. They shook hands briefly. "I know this guy at the Air Station in Alameda," he continued. "I'm bettin' he could get me a flight to one of the Naval Air Stations on the East Coast."

They found Lieutenant Rosetto on the bridge, and with Martin's help, Scotty was able to tell his story and make his request for the emergency leave. He was granted fifteen days.

"But remember this," the Executive Officer said. "You must be back on board this ship by the end of the fifteen days regardless of any circumstances. We'll be lucky if they let us stay in this port that long. Now you'd better shake a leg and work on getting that flight."

Scotty was elated, and after packing a few things in his duffel bag, he left for Alameda.

"Good luck, and give Margaret my best," Martin yelled as Scotty descended the short gang plank to the dock. Then he hurried back to the mess hall and opened Angela's letters. They were warm and cheerful, open and sincere, and it was a joy to read her words. They were touching words of love and affection, exuding hope and faith in the future. She knew that some day they would be together again, then they would decide if they could have a life of happiness together. But she knew how it was with Navy men. She had known other Navy men besides her brother Frank and they all had the same problems when they were serving aboard a Navy ship; sea-duty did strange things to them, and complicated their lives.

Strange, he thought, he knew her for such a short time, he knew so little about her, and yet, reading her letters, he felt the kinship of their hearts and minds. Their sexual union had been the ultimate in nature's insistent design and it gave a depth to their relationship that goes beyond human understanding. He knew without a doubt that there could never be anyone else in his life like Angela. The memory of that one night with her was engraved in his mind, ready for immediate recall whenever he wanted to think of something uplifting and beautiful.

SEVENTEEN

San Francisco!

Martin knew there had to be something very unusual going on as soon as he saw there was a letter from Fred. His mother's letters were saying basically the same thing, but hers was more in the way of a complaint. "Your father is working himself to death. He is at the plant from early morning to late at night and he is beginning to look awful. He is also drinking too much and with everything as it is, he's probably ruining his health. I wish you would write to him and tell him to take it easy. He seems to listen to you more than any of the rest of us."

Fred's letter was more to the point. "As soon as you have served your one year in the Navy I wish you would plan to come back home and work with us here at the plant. A couple of weeks ago Dad had an attack of some kind, either a slight heart attack or a small stroke. He got over it all right, but the doctor says that was a warning and that Dad must slow down."

"We have so many orders for rifle bullets, we have had to purchase many new presses and we have set up new assembly areas all over the place. We ran out of manufacturing space, so Dad bought three more adjoining farms. This not only gives us more buildings to set up shell assemblies, but it also reduces the possibility of injuring other people or damaging other peoples' property in case of accidental explosions. We've had three bad ones in the past several months which would have been less severe if we hadn't had so much gun powder stored in one place. In other words, we are decentralizing shell assembly by acquiring more land and more buildings. Whenever a neighbor complains about the noise or about the potential danger of explosions, Dad just offers them a good price for their property. With prices way up like they are, so far they have all accepted his offers, and now we are even having people come to us with offers to sell. Incidentally, with all the farm land we are acquiring it was necessary to set up a Farm Operations Department and we have hired an excellent manager to take charge of that. If this war in Europe ever ends, I wouldn't mind taking charge of the farm operations myself."

"But all of this additional business and expansion of our production capacity is driving us crazy. We don't have enough supervisors and managers. We can get all the women production assembly workers we want, but we really need foremen, supervisors and managers. I can only do so much myself, and I don't think Dad is going to hold up under the strain much longer."

"That's why we want you to come back here and help us as soon as you can. You can start right out at the top, helping me and Dad, and at a good salary. Money is no problem. I understand you are making about $36.00 a month in the Navy. We could start you out at $36.00 a day or more, any amount you want right now--you wouldn't believe the money we're taking in! So right now anyone in the family can earn as much as they want. I have written to Margaret and asked her to come back and work here also. But she seems to be upset about something at present and hasn't given me an answer as yet. We might as well make all we can now, because who knows how long the war in Europe and this kind of business will last. Remember what Grandpop used to always be telling us when we were kids, 'Make hay while the sun shines.' Well, right now the sun is shining brightly. We have many excellent contacts with the federal government at the present time because of our ability to produce the ammunition they need and I'm sure we could get you a draft exemption. We have even gotten draft exemptions for some of our employees because our business is so essential to the government's defense effort."

"Besides it is silly for you to be out there riding around on a tug boat when you could be contributing much more to your country right here. Growing up around Dad's business of making explosives, gun powder and rifle bullets has given us an opportunity that few other people have, and we are stupid not to take advantage of it. You know Dad always did fairly well with the business. But he worked hard all of his life for peanuts compared to what we are doing now. If the war in Europe keeps going and if we play our cards right, we should be able to pile up enough profits to make us one of the richest families in the state. You are the only one that can make the decision for you. So please let me know as soon as you have made a decision one way or another."

"What I have written you here is my own opinion of what I think would be best for you and the rest of us. But besides all that, Dad asked me to tell you he would like you to come home and work with us. He would like you to learn the business and be part of the family operation. In addition to that, I think he really misses you and is

probably worried that you'll get involved in actual warfare
and get yourself hurt or killed. He reads all those newspapers, you know, and the war news is all bad, and now
he is saying he thinks Roosevelt is trying to get us into the
war. And I think maybe he is right. Hope to hear from
you soon."

Martin put Fred's letter back into its envelope and laid
it aside. Margaret's letter was the shortest of them all. She
merely said she hoped everything was going well for him,
she was thinking of taking a job at Dad's plant and moving
back home, and would he please tell Scotty to write to her.

With all the pressure that these letters from his family
put on him, for a fleeting moment, Martin had another one
of those onslaughts of doubts and regrets--maybe the
whole direction he had chosen for his life was all wrong--
but there was no one else to blame--he had made all of the
choices--the decision to study for the ministry--becoming
disenchanted with that--deciding to join the Navy and
then the thing with Jim Johnson--maybe he should have
majored in chemistry and gone to work at the plant--but,
my God, just the thought of working with gun powder and
bullets--that was absolutely revolting--no, there had to be
more to life than that!

He put the letters away and prepared to go back on
watch, his last before starting the next day on his three-day
liberty in the city of San Francisco. There would be much
to see there, and he hoped, much to do. The anticipation
of liberty in San Francisco, the exciting city of the Golden
Gate Bridge which he had heard so much about, left him in
no mood to think seriously about answering those letters
from his family or from Alice. He would attend to that
later.

The next day as he left the ship with the liberty party and headed for Market Street one of his shipmates caught up with him and walked with him. "You going to take the cable car up town?" It was Lefty Flagner, the signalman from his watch on the bridge.

"Yes," Martin answered. "In fact, that's what I am going to do first thing in San Francisco. I'm going to ride it to the end and back again just for the fun of it. A friend of mine told me it was great fun and something I should be sure to do if I ever visited here." Then he remembered it was Alice who told him about her trip to San Francisco, and he thought about the letter he had just received from her. He couldn't believe she had chosen to stay with that professor under the circumstances. Logically it was O. K., but emotionally it would be hard to take, he thought. But they probably did me a big favor, under the circumstances. He quickly pushed these thoughts from his mind just as Flagner was saying, "Good, I'll ride with you."

Martin was glad for the company. They rode to the end of the line where the cable car turned around and headed back in the direction from which it came.

"I hear there is a servicemen's center in the downtown area, called the NSO, the National Service Organization, where you can find out where to go and what there is to do," Flagner said. "They have shows and dances and all kinds of activities for servicemen. Think we should check it out?"

"Sounds good to me," Martin answered. "Let's go."

They found the NSO, and after checking on various sight-seeing tours they had lunch. It was good to be in the presence of women and girls again after weeks on the ship and good to be eating food that had not come from the ship's galley.

Martin spotted a row of public telephones in the lobby of the NSO building, and he suddenly had a strong urge to call Angela. He got a pocket full of coins at the service counter and then stepped into one of the booths and dialed the operator. He called her at her home telephone number, person to person, because he knew she was at work, and when her mother answered, he had the operator ask for the number where she could be reached. It was already late afternoon in New York.

"How are you, Angela?" he asked when she answered.

"Who is this?"

"This is lonesome Martin Miller calling from San Francisco."

"Oh, Martin, this is a pleasant surprise!" I didn't expect to hear from you by phone. I only had one letter from you and I was expecting more."

"Angela, I love you and I miss you, and I wish you were here with me. So I couldn't pass up the chance to call you."

"I love you too, Martin. I'd love to be with you too. I hear you are only going to be there a short time or I would get the train and come out there. Scotty came back, you know. He flew all the way by Navy plane, and guess what? He and Margaret have gone to Elkton, Maryland, to get married. Then they're going to get the train from Baltimore and spend their honeymoon in a Pullman car on the way back to San Francisco. Margaret is taking a month's leave of absence. I understand your mother and father were very upset because they are not having a church wedding back home. But they just didn't have enough time."

"Well, thanks for the latest news. I was thinking of calling home to find out how they were doing. Scotty sure did make it back in a hurry."

"Yes, they said he got a flight immediately, through Chicago, and he was here in N. Y. a couple of days after he left Alameda. Margaret said she is thinking about giving up the apartment in New York and going home to have the baby, and then taking a job at your Dad's plant. And, she says she wants me to go along and get a job there too. What do you think of that?"

"There's a rumor that we're going to Hawaii from here, and it looks like it will be a long time until we see each other again. This is an almost impossible situation, and it's not fair to you, so I don't want you to feel obligated to wait for me. It's up to you, if you know what I mean."

"Oh, Martin, let's not talk about that. But I suppose we'll have to face reality, especially if you are going to Hawaii. I hear there are lots of beautiful girls over there."

"Well, I'm not planning on any Hawaiian girls. But you're right, we have to face reality," he said. "I have no idea when I'll get to see you again."

"I love you, Martin. But I know a lot about sailors and I know I can't expect you to feel obligated either. I just hope your ship comes back to the states soon. In the meantime you just try to stay healthy and happy, and try to remember me."

"I'll always love you, Angela, and you know why. But I have to hang up now, I'm running out of change. Let's keep on writing each other. Good-bye Angela," Martin said sadly.

"Good-bye, love," Angela said. "Good-bye."

As he hung up the telephone, Martin felt much better. He and Angela had an understanding. Their experience together had bound their hearts together forever, but in the realities of their separate existences, they would not bind each other in an obligation to a relationship in an uncertain future.

"Hey, Flagner." Martin called out to his shipmate as he walked across the lobby toward him. "Let's go dancing and have some fun. It's no fun having a girl back home."

"Yeah, I know," said Flagner. "I'm married."

They went into the main hall, or ballroom of the NSO where a dance was in progress with a live volunteer band providing the music. They listened to the music and watched the dancing for awhile. There were many more servicemen than there were girls and it was necessary to cut in if you wanted to dance. Flagner didn't hesitate. He cut in on a soldier and danced with a good-looking, tall blonde. But very soon he was cut in on by another sailor.

Martin sat on the side lines for quite some time, and enjoyed watching the others on the dance floor. He spotted a girl who reminded him of Angela. He kept watching her as one after another of the servicemen cut in. Finally he walked out on the dance floor and asked her to dance. She was a natural follower, and they danced well together. She was very young. Even though she did remind him of Angela, she was much younger, probably just out of high school, but she was fully developed and very attractive.

They danced, and danced some more. It really wasn't fair. It was in fact against the rules. Other servicemen would look but then hesitate to cut in. Maybe it was because of Martin's size, or maybe it was the way she looked like she wanted to dance only with him, but no one cut in.

They danced every type of dance to every number that was played for quite some time. Finally the scheduled dance ended and the band left. They went to the snack bar for cookies and a soft drink.

"I'm sorry, I didn't introduce myself out on the floor, I was enjoying it so much. I'm Martin Miller. What's your name?"

"Julie Enderson," she answered coyly.

"I thought you would have an Italian name. You look Italian."

"Well, you're close. My mother is of Italian descent, but not my father. My father doesn't know where his ancestors came from. He thinks they came here from back east with the gold rush and just stayed. But he's definitely not Italian."

"I was wondering if you would join me for dinner and a movie tonight," Martin said, surprised at his own boldness.

"I'm sorry, we are not allowed to date the servicemen. It's against the rules."

"Oh, I didn't know. That's too bad, at least for me," he said.

"There is a way we can get around that rule, though," Julie said mischievously.

"How's that?"

"Well, if an NSO volunteer's parents, I'm an NSO volunteer, if her parents invite you to their home, then we are allowed to see you off premises. We don't call it a date. But some of the girls get some very nice dates that way."

Martin looked her squarely in the eyes. He was completely intrigued now. "Do you think your parents would invite me to your house?"

"I think my mother would invite you. I'll call her. She picks me up anyhow. She can tell the chaperones." She led the way over to the telephones.

While Julie was using the telephone, Flagner walked up to them. "I'll see you back on the ship, Miller," he said. "I've been invited to go roller skating with a group here. I saw that you were getting involved so I didn't butt in. See you later."

"O. K.," Martin said. "Thanks. See you later."

EIGHTEEN

An Unexpected Invitation

Julie made the arrangements, and in less than an hour her mother arrived and got their attention on the dance floor where they were dancing to the music of the jukebox.

"This is Martin Miller, Mother. Martin, this is my mother," Julia said, trying to be very proper.

"I'm pleased to meet you, Mrs. Enderson," Martin said.

"I'm pleased to meet you," she answered, looking him over carefully. "I have dinner started at home. I wasn't expecting company, so there's nothing special, but you are welcome to have dinner with us, if you would like to. Julie says she told you about the rules we have here, and I'm on the board of directors, so I would like to invite you to our home."

"That's very nice of you," he said. "I would like very much to join you." He liked her immediately.

"Fine," she said. "My car is out on the street about a block from here."

They left the NSO building and walked to Mrs. Enderson's car. It was a large, four-door, 1939 model Buick. They drove only a few minutes before they passed the Mark Hopkins Hotel. Martin stretched his neck in order to get a better look at it.

"I've heard about that place," he said. "A friend of mine from college told me about the place they have on the top."

"Oh, the Top of the Marks, that's one of my favorite spots," said Mrs. Enderson.

"I don't like that place," said Julie. "They won't let me go up to the Top, without my mother. That makes me so mad."

"Well, you're just too young, Julie, dear," said her mother. "You'll be old enough, soon enough."

"Maybe we can go there later. My mother also likes to dance. Right, Mother?"

"Now, Julie," her mother said.

Martin was intrigued by the casual relationship between the mother and daughter.

A short time later they pulled up in front of the house. It was a big old Victorian house, in a neighborhood of spacious yards and old trees and shrubs. When they entered, a maid took Martin's white Navy hat.

Dinner was almost formal. He couldn't believe it. It was supervised by Mrs. Enderson, but served by the maid. It was just the three of them. Red table wine was served, Italian style, during the whole meal. Martin began to feel the effects of the wine by the time dessert was served. He wasn't accustomed to drinking that much, and by the time they had finished he was completely relaxed.

"Is your father at work?" Martin asked Julie.

"My father is an officer in the Navy. He's in Pearl Harbor at present. He's on some admiral's staff and they are on board one of the flagships out there. We just had a letter from him yesterday."

"Yes, we hardly ever see him anymore," Mrs. Enderson said. "He used to be stationed here in San Francisco. But then he got promoted and now he is away most of the time. We haven't seen him for almost a year now," she added as pensiveness crept into her facial expression. But she didn't say any more.

After dinner, Julie went to the piano and started playing. She played a classical number or two and then switched to modern jazz numbers, then back again to classical. The maid served an after dinner drink. In the middle of a number, Julie was interrupted by the maid to answer the telephone. She came back into the room shortly and announced: "I'm sorry, Martin, I forgot I had tentatively promised a special friend I would go out with him tonight."

"Oh, Julie, that's horrible," her mother said. "That's very impolite. You should have asked to be excused because you have a guest."

"This is somebody special, Mother," Julie snapped. "It's Bobby, and you know I can't miss seeing him." Turning to Martin she said, "I really am sorry. Maybe I'll see you again at the NSO or something."

"Oh, that's O. K. That's O. K.," Martin said quickly. "I've enjoyed every minute of it, visiting with you, and I don't want to interfere with any other plans. I'm grateful for your hospitality. You've been more than kind, already, getting your mother to bring me along home and entertaining me and all."

"Mother will see to it that you get back to your ship or wherever you're going. Won't you, Mother?"

"Of course, Julie."

In a few minutes a horn sounded out front, and Julie dashed off, shouting a good-bye as she went through the door.

"This is embarrassing," Mrs. Enderson said. "But I'll have to admit, it has happened before." She called the maid and had her bring in a bottle of champagne.

"What are your plans? Are you going back to your ship tonight?" she then asked.

"No," said Martin. "In fact I was planning to get a hotel room or maybe stay at the YMCA. I'm on a three-day liberty. I was thinking I would like to see the Top of the Marks, and maybe I can get a room there."

"I'll be more than happy to take you to the Marks, but I would like to freshen up and relax a bit before we go, if that's all right with you."

"You don't have to do that, Mrs. Enderson. I can just call a cab. I appreciate your hospitality."

The maid came into the living room and announced that everything was cleared away, and it was time for her to leave. She said good night and left.

Mrs. Enderson got up from the chair in which she had been sitting, picked up the bottle of champagne and walked slowly toward the sofa on which Martin was sitting. He followed her movements and saw her for the first time while she was pouring the sparkling wine into his glass. She was built just like Julie, but a little heavier. She was older, of course, but not really old--thirty- eight or thirty-nine, he guessed. She too had the same dark, seductive look about her that reminded him of Angela. He could feel the flow of chemistry reacting between them as she looked directly into his eyes.

He had wondered and even fantasized what it might be like to have an older woman and this possibility now took possession of his conscious thoughts. He got up and turned up the radio which was playing a slow dance tune.

"Would you like to dance?" he asked.

"I'd love to," she answered, sliding gracefully into his arms. He held her close as they danced through several slow numbers, then she pulled away and reached for the iced champagne bottle.

"Would you like to freshen up?" she asked, as she finished pouring more champagne.

Martin knew what she meant. "Yes," he said. "I'd like that very much."

They went upstairs to a plush bedroom with its own tiled bathroom.

"I really do need a shower, Mrs. Enderson," Martin said.

"Good, I'll take one with you. But, please, call me Jean."

His heart raced madly as they undressed and showered. As they soaped one another they massaged playfully, and then rinsed in stimulating hot water. They dried off with luxuriously large white towels, and he followed Jean into her bed. There they embraced tenderly, deliberately and Jean guided and encouraged Martin in the mutual exchange of titillating kisses as they indulged in the mutual enjoyment of their clean, naked bodies. Finally they shifted to a mutually comfortable position and as he entered her she was warm and receptive. The maturity and the expertise of her response was a new experience for Martin. His youth and virility seemed to be a sheer delight to this thoroughly feminine and responsive woman.

When it was over, Jean said, "Martin, dear boy, you have no idea how necessary and enjoyable that was. I wonder if you have any idea how masculine and attractive you are to a woman. Julie and I were both being attracted to you as if you were a strong magnet. It was fortunate for all of us that her friend called when he did. It's better for

Julie that she didn't get more involved with you and better for you that you didn't risk getting her into trouble, and infinitely better for me; I use a diaphragm, so you don't have to worry. I feel like saying thanks, Martin."

"I'm the one to say thanks. You've done a lot for me, a lot more than you may know," he said, as he pressed her with one last meaningful montage of hugs and kisses. Then he dozed off into peaceful, dreamless sleep.

NINETEEN

An Enlightening Experience

Later, Martin felt the gentle massaging of Jean's delicate fingers and the wetness of her kisses as she slowly awakened him.

"Boy, that sure was a short night," he said, yawning and stretching.

"I know," Jean answered. "But we'll have to get dressed and get out of here before Julie comes back. It's eleven thirty."

"Eleven thirty! Oh, I thought it was morning," he said, still yawning.

"I wish we could spend the rest of the night, but, I don't know what Julie would do if she found out about this. We'll have to go now."

"Can we still make it to the Top of the Marks? I sure would like to see that and maybe I can get a room there. Then you won't have to drive anywhere else."

"Without reservations, I don't know. Besides, it's very expensive there."

"I have enough money. I guess I don't have to worry about that," he said, thinking about Fred's last letter.

"Oh, wonderful," Jean said. "Most sailors have to worry about money. My husband was an enlisted man before he got the appointment to the Academy."

"I didn't know you could do that--I mean go from the enlisted ranks into the Naval academy," Martin said.

"I guess it's not easy. But he did it. He ran away from home and joined the Navy, but later he was reconciled with his family. His father was involved in politics in Nevada and had a fortune which he had inherited from his gold mining ancestors. His father couldn't stand him being an enlisted man, so about a year or so after he enlisted, this appointment came through. That's where I met him. I was born and raised in Maryland. We were married after he graduated--my God, that was eighteen years ago and most of those years have been lonely years. I hope you're not planning to make the Navy a career."

"No, I wasn't planning that. I guess I was really just anticipating the draft, and basically, I guess I just wanted to get away for a year to get a new perspective, more or less. I was a ministerial student or pre-theological, as some call it. Originally I had planned to go on to the Seminary, and become a minister."

"Really! Well, for heaven's sake. A minister, my God. I hope I haven't led you astray or something."

"No, don't worry about that. And besides, I'm not a minister, not yet, at least, but that's a long story."

They drove to the Mark Hopkins Hotel. There were no single rooms available, but he took a two room suite, which was the only thing available and for which he had to pay in advance. He cashed the cashier's check which his father had secretly slipped to him while he was home on boot leave. "Stick this in your wallet for an emergency," his father had said. Martin assumed it was his enlisted man's uniform and his duffel bag baggage what caused the manager to have some doubts about his ability to pay.

Then they took the elevator to the Top of the Marks lounge. They ordered champagne and then stood by the rail at the glass wall from which they took in the spectacular view of the city, with its countless lights, backed by the magnificent bay.

"I must ask you something, Martin," Jean said, as soon as they had relaxed. "Do you think I am a terrible person for doing what we did back at the house? You know what I mean--everything we did. I guess I'm just as bad as the rest of them now. I've never done that before, but, with you, it seemed so right."

"Believe me, I don't think anything bad about you. It was a beautiful experience," Martin said.

"Well, I'm beginning to get some funny feelings about it now that it is over. I know I should feel like a real, low down, dirty adulteress, no better than what I used to think of any of the other cheating Navy wives, not that they all do it, understand. But Martin, I don't. I don't feel that way. I know that fornication is wrong, adultery is wrong, deviate sex is wrong, cheating is wrong. But if this is true, if this is the truth, then why don't I now feel that they are wrong? Why don't I feel the remorse. Why do I feel instead, like shouting to my friends and neighbors, hey, you should try this, it's great." Jean paused to catch her breath and take a drink of the champagne. Then she continued, "What did you mean at home when you said that I did more for you than what I know? What did you mean by that?"

Martin studied her for several minutes while he collected his thoughts, for he had not as yet formulated words, or sentences to convey the concept he had in mind. "I think I had something similar in mind," he said, hesitatingly. "I believe I was thinking that you have helped me learn something very important. You have made it possible for me to experience adultery, and I have willingly participated in causing you to become an adulteress. I guess, I had always believed that anyone who committed adultery should be condemned, period, because the commandment is: 'Thou shalt not commit adultery.' But I can see now that there are times and circumstances when adultery may be humanly necessary, that the wording of the commandment is too simple. Yes, that's it, it is oversimplification at its worst. It might have been stated better 'Thou shalt not commit adultery except in this or that case, or unless ...' Do you see what I mean? Whoever wrote those words did not do justice to a loving and forgiving God, and consequently left future generations hanging and forever condemned. But, then, I suppose this is another example of what Jesus was trying to teach, forgiveness of sins--'let he who is without sin cast the first stone.' Maybe that's what it is all about."

He looked into Jean's face and saw tears forming in the corners of her eyes. "Oh, Martin," she said, and then burst into muffled, silent weeping.

"I'm sorry, Jean," Martin said. "I guess I've done it again. I guess I get carried away whenever I'm trying to put ideas into words, especially when it is about something that has been bothering me. I'm sorry." He lifted the champagne glass and drank it down in several large gulps.

"No, no, don't be sorry," Jean said. "I want to thank you for that explanation," she said. "You have no idea how I've struggled with the guilt of wanting to make love, of needing companionship and love and sex, of trying to convince myself that it is wrong even if my husband is away for months and months. I was crying now because it was such a relief to hear you say that it's not all absolutely, positively, black or white, wrong."

"Well, that's how you helped me more than you realized," Martin said, slurring the words. The alcohol was taking effect. "I guess we've both learned something from our experience, but I'm not sure anyone else would agree with my explanation. I certainly won't be able to express that opinion if I ever want to become a Lutheran minister."

"Oh, my God, no," Jean said, laughing nervously. "The little church I used to belong to back home would hang you for an explanation like that. But I think you're right and it is a shame that subjects like this can't be discussed more openly."

"There does seem to be some irreconcilable differences between the church's teachings and the natural sexual needs and desires of most human beings. I suspect that's because some of the precepts of the church were formulated in ancient times, and also in the early days of the Christian church, and some of these precepts have been taken for eternal laws. But are they? Some of these precepts may no longer be relevant."

"You're probably right," Jean mused. "But, . . ."

"And," Martin interrupted. "it's my guess that's what's causing so many church members to profess allegiance to their religion, but then quietly living out their lives according to the dictates of their own best experience and judgement, ignoring the teachings of the church. In other words, it's the cause of the hypocrisy which has become so widespread in our society."

"And maybe the hypocrisy causes the guilt," mused Jean.

"Yes," Martin said, "just think of the suffering this must be causing, the frustration, the anger, and as you have said, the guilt."

"My goodness, we really have gotten into some deep water here, haven't we?" Jean said. She looked around to see if Martin's overly loud recitation had attracted an audience, but no one was paying any attention. "Would you like to dance?" she asked. "There is a small dance floor over there in the corner."

"O. K. I'm sorry, I did it again. I do get carried away, don't I?" Martin said, blushing somewhat.

"Yes, you do. But I can understand why."

"Let's dance," said Martin.

As they danced, Jean whispered in Martin's ear, "Do you have a special girlfriend back home?"

The question prompted memories of Alice as she was back on campus, and their engagement after graduation, and her letters. But immediately, the pain of those memories caused him to turn them off, and he switched his thoughts to Angela, but then a picture of Pamia entered in, and then, the trinity, Alice, Angela, and Pamia, the three-in-one, representing the one perfect woman, whirled around in his head. The champagne was beginning to affect his thinking. Finally, after some delay, he answered, "Yes, I have a very special girl. Her name is Angela," he stammered, having almost said 'Alice.'

"Are you in love with her?"

"Very much."

"She must be very nice."

"You remind me of her."

"Was she a school mate?"

"No. I only knew her for two days, in New York."

"She must be very special."

"Yes, very special. I'll always love her."

The memory of Angela now became vivid in his mind's eye. With Angela his appetite had been whetted. He had experienced with her the ultimate which satisfies a man's eternal hunger and he knew that forever after he would be in quest of that ultimate which would satisfy his enormous appetite.

Now as they danced the chemistry began to react again between them and their bodies blended together in rhythmic swaying until the music stopped. Martin held Jean momentarily as the couples left the floor.

"Let's go down to my room," he whispered into her ear.

"It's very late, Martin," she answered, resisting.

"Stay for just a little while," he coaxed, as they walked back to the oval bar and had one last drink.

"I'm sorry, Martin," she said. "I should never have encouraged you like I did earlier tonight. But what happened, happened and we can't change that now. Let's just both put this night into our memories as a beautiful and enlightening experience, which I think is what it is, and let it go at that."

"You're right, Jean," Martin said, suddenly realizing that he had become overbearing, and that she had saved him from making a complete fool of himself. "This was a beautiful and enlightening experience and I'll never forget it, or you."

Jean looked up into Martin's eyes now and held them while she transmitted to him an acknowledgment of understanding that cannot be communicated from one person to another in any other way. "I really must go now," she said.

He accompanied her to the elevator and rode along down to the lobby. There, as they embraced one last time, Martin said, "Tell Julie good-bye for me, will you?"

"I'll tell her. Good-bye, Martin," she said. Then she went out through the huge revolving door.

"Good-bye," he said, and he turned immediately and headed back up to his room, trying to remember as he went, where he had read, or who had written, those beautiful words: "To meet, to love, and then to pass on, there is no greater glory."

TWENTY

A Board of Inquiry

The next day Martin slept in. The afternoon sun came in brightly through the windows of the little parlor of his suite as he awakened, and this contrasted with the darkness of the bedroom where he had drawn all of the drapes. It also contrasted with the despondency which had enveloped him, and it accelerated the throbbing in his head. He got up slowly and deliberately, grunting and moaning with each movement of his body. After he made it to the bathroom, he took a long and extremely hot shower and then finished off with the water as cold as he could stand it.

Slowly the events of the past day and night came back into coherent focus. He thought of the ironic, short, swift relationship. It had been a beautiful, enriching experience. They had met and loved and learned together. But now it was nothing but a warm memory, which left him again with that sense of loss that invariably accompanied an enlargement of his circle of awareness.

He went down to the hotel dining room for lunch. Eating alone like this, he realized that he missed the company of his friend Scotty. He liked to be with people. His thoughts then turned to Alice. She was going to have a baby--his baby. This was a fact of life he just couldn't ignore. In spite of his involvement with other women, Alice was a part of his life, but married to someone else. He longed to be with her, to sit down with her, and straighten things out with one of their long talks. He realized now the impossibility of loving someone and at the same time serving duty aboard a Navy ship. Angela was right, sea-duty does strange things to you, he thought, it complicates your life.

He ate heartily of the roast prime rib of beef, baked potato, assorted vegetables, apple pie and plenty of bread and butter and coffee. Then he checked out of the hotel and, on foot, headed for the docks to return to his ship. The food and the exercise brought back vitality, and by the time he got back he was in high spirits again. He saluted as he walked across the short gang plank and stepped aboard his ship. Immediately the O.D. called out his name, "Martin Miller, you are to report to the Executive Officer at once."

"I'm not due back aboard until tomorrow at 1300 hours, Sir," Martin replied, somewhat startled by this unexpected attention.

"He left word for you to report immediately upon boarding, Miller. I wouldn't question the Exec. if I were you."

"Aye, aye, Sir," Martin said to the young Ensign. "Is he on the bridge, Sir?"

"Try the wardroom."

"Aye, aye, Sir."

He went immediately to the wardroom and stuck his head through the hatchway. Lieutenant Rosetto was pouring a cup of coffee for himself. A cigarette hung from his mouth. He looked up and said, "Martin, you're back early. Come in please."

"Good afternoon, Lieutenant. I talked with Angela yesterday and she said I should give you her regards. And she said I should tell you to write sometime."

"Yeah, I'm a lousy correspondent. But thanks for the message."

"You left orders for me to report to you as soon as I got back aboard, Sir."

"Yes, Martin, there's a new development on the Johnson thing. I made some discreet inquiries, as I promised you, through Navy friends of mine in Norfolk, and because of those inquiries, somehow or other word got around that there was something suspicious about Johnson's death, especially with his parents pushing for more information. Then a Navy Board of Inquiry was set up to investigate the case. So far they have taken a deposition from the sailor he was with, a guy named George Lundy who is stationed at the Naval Air Station at Norfolk. He was drunk and shooting off his mouth, one night in a bar, about being in a fight and getting away from the SPs, and one of those SPs happened to be at the bar, off-duty. In his deposition Lundy made the statement that they were in a fight with a seaman from our ship. But to make a long story short, agents from the Naval Investigations office here in San Francisco are coming aboard tomorrow. They are going to question all personnel who were on liberty from our ship that night in Norfolk."

"Oh, Jesus!" Martin exclaimed. "I thought this would happen."

"Well, you remember I told you to forget it--but now, the cat's out of the bag. I hate to say, I told you so, but if you had just let it alone . . . trying to find out if an autopsy was made, that probably opened up the whole thing, especially with his parents pushing."

"But, look," Lieutenant Rosetto continued, "this gives me another problem. When you are questioned, you will have to answer truthfully and then they'll want a deposition, and you'll be under oath. But remember you told me of your involvement confidentially, and even though, technically, as an officer, I should have made a report of your involvement, I didn't betray your confidence. Now, Martin, it's your turn; you cannot tell anyone that you told me of your involvement. If you do, I'll be in trouble."

"But, if they ask me, I'd have to lie under oath in order to protect you. I don't know if I can do that."

"Martin, I gave you my word that I would not mention anything to anyone about your involvement. Now you have to give me your word that you will not implicate me. Do you understand that?"

"Yes, Sir, I understand. But then I would have to deny any involvement at all, under oath," Martin said, and remembering Scotty's advice in the beginning, wondered if that's what he should do. "But I couldn't get away with that. This enlisted man who was with Johnson, this George Lundy, he could probably identify me."

Then after some thought, he said, "Lieutenant, to tell you the truth I am fed up with worrying about being implicated in Johnson's death. I have worried myself sick about it, but I didn't try to kill him. If anybody killed him, he did it himself. He was drunk and disorderly, antagonistic and violent, acting like a fool. I am going to get this off my mind once and for all, Lieutenant. I'm going to tell them everything I know about it and let the chips fall where they may!" He was using one of his father's favorite expressions. "But there is no reason I have to tell anyone I discussed it with you, Sir. That conversation was strictly between you and me. It was confidential and no one has to know about it. I would like to assure you, Sir, that I'll never tell anyone about it. I give you my word on that."

"Fine, Martin. That's the only honorable thing to do. I just wanted to make sure we understood each other on that."

TWENTY-ONE

An Incriminating Deposition

When the questioning of those who had been on liberty in Norfolk the night of Johnson's death was in progress, Martin was extremely curious. He paid close attention and listened carefully. The questioning took place in the Mess Hall where all hands who had been on liberty that night in Norfolk had been gathered. Two agents had come aboard. One of the agents asked all of the questions and the other listened and took notes. The agent asked only three questions:

(1) Were you on liberty in Norfolk, Virginia, on the night of 27 September, 1941?

(2) Did you see James P. Johnson, Boatswain's Mate First Class that night?

(3) If so, where was he and what was he doing?

The first six men questioned answered "yes" to the first question, and "no" to the second question, and therefore did not have to answer the third or any further questions and were immediately excused. Martin was the seventh person to be questioned, and as he stepped up in front of the agents he was sweating profusely.

"We are asking questions here for a Board of Inquiry being conducted in Norfolk, Virginia, in connection with the death of James P. Johnson, Boatswain's Mate First Class, on 27 September 1941. Do you understand that this is an official Navy Investigation and that perjury is subject to punishment under Naval Regulations?"

"Yes, Sir, I do," Martin answered.

"Were you on liberty in the city of Norfolk, Virginia on the night of 27 September 1941?

"Yes, Sir, I was," Martin said.

"Did you see Boatswain's Mate First Class James P. Johnson while in the city of Norfolk, Virginia, on that night?

"Yes, Sir, I did," Martin answered quietly.

"Where was he and what was he doing when you saw him," the agent asked.

"It was at the White Front Restaurant on Granby Street. He was at the counter, and he was arguing with another Navy enlisted man," Martin answered calmly.

Both of the agents' eyes came alive, and excitement showed in their faces. They immediately put him under oath and proceeded to take his deposition. They repeated the first three questions and then continued with the following:

"Did you know the enlisted man he was arguing with?"

"I met him earlier that day. I saw him and Johnson earlier that day at a bar. He was introduced to me as Lundy."

"What were they arguing about?"

"Something about a woman they had been dancing with."

"What happened after that? Did they leave the restaurant?"

"Well, yes, Sir, they left after the Shore Patrol came. They left with the Shore Patrol."

"The Shore Patrol?"

"Yes, they both got into a fight with another enlisted man, at the counter, and the SPs came in and broke it up, and the SPs took them all out of the restaurant."

"Did you know this other enlisted man?"

Martin hesitated momentarily, but then answered, "Yes, Sir. It was me. I was the other enlisted man."

The agents looked at one another in disbelief. They conferred in whispers and searched through some papers they had with them in a brief case. Then they continued the questioning.

"Did you strike James Johnson about the face and head?"

Martin knew this was a crucial question. He thought over his answer carefully. "After they attacked me, I defended myself with several right and left punches. But it was at this point that I noticed Johnson had a very strange look on his face, and I held back. The SPs came in about this time and stopped us."

"Did the SPs strike Johnson?"

"No, Sir. At least I didn't see them hit him. They merely grabbed his arms."

With further questioning by the agents, Martin gave them the rest of the details of the incident. They conferred briefly with Captain Mills, and Lieutenant Rosetto, and left the ship.

About a week later Lieutenant Rosetto took Martin aside on the wing off of the bridge to talk to him.

"I got word from my friends in Norfolk that it's possible the Board of Inquiry is going to recommend you for a General Court Martial. The only evidence they have is the fight you had with Johnson at the White Front Restaurant, with several witnesses besides Lundy. Your deposition was self-incriminating. But it's not definite as yet, they say they've still got some additional checking to do. It may take a long time yet."

Afterwards, Martin went down to his bunk in the crew's quarters to think about what Rosetto had just told him. There was no denying that he was involved in the events which ended in Johnson's death. It made him look guilty, and that's why he felt guilty, but there was the strange look on Johnson's face; and there was something that Cathy had said in her letter. Yes, what was it? He dug out her letter, and there it was: "I feel so guilty about his death, because it was that night that I left him at the tavern and got you to walk me to the Portsmouth Ferry, and then you came out to the house later. I keep wondering if that made him drink more and get so drunk that maybe it aggravated his condition."

"What condition?" Martin said aloud to himself.

He had to have an answer to that question, and he had not answered Cathy's letter as yet. But since there wouldn't be time to get a letter to her and receive a reply before sailing, on his next liberty, he found a telephone booth along the street just off of Fisherman's Wharf and, prepared with plenty of coins, he called her. She was still living with her parents, and he found her at home.

"Oh, hello, Martin, I'm so glad to hear from you. How are you?"

"I'm fine," he said, "except that I'm having some problems with the fact that I was in a fight with Jim Johnson the night he died." He brought her up to date on the latest developments as quickly as he could.

"Well, I didn't know it was you when I asked if you knew anything about him being in a fight with another enlisted man from your ship. But I was hoping I would hear from you."

"Cathy, the reason I'm calling is because you mentioned something about Johnson having some condition."

"Oh, yes, well, Jim did tell me one time, after a few drinks that he was having some kind of a heart problem that the pharmacist's mate had discovered and wanted him to go to see the Naval base doctor about. But Jim got the pharmacist's mate on your ship to keep it out of his medical record, and he didn't go to see the doctor on the base, because he had plans of staying in the Navy until he could retire. He didn't want to get a medical discharge. When he told me he said he wanted to tell me a secret and I had to promise that I would never tell anyone. But now-- he's dead. I guess I should have told his parents. But they were so upset and I was so upset, and I had promised Jim, I just couldn't say anything during the funeral."

"Cathy, believe it or not, but this is something of what I suspected. I saw this strange look on his face when we were, ah, when he was attacking me. Look, Cathy, do me a great favor. This is very important to me. Call Johnson's parents and tell them what you have told me, and ask them to request that an autopsy be performed on him. Maybe you could take time off and go see them again, but try your best to get them to do it. I know it is asking a lot, but do you think you could do that for me?"

"Oh, my God, Martin, you know what that means? He's been buried for over a month. And I'll still feel it was my fault because . . "

"Cathy, for God's sake listen to me! You've got to get that notion out of you head completely. You had absolutely nothing to do with his death and neither did I. He would have done what he did and died even if you and I had never existed. Jim Johnson was not a good man, and you recognized that when you left him that day in Norfolk and went home. Maybe he didn't deserve to die, but he brought it on all by himself, without any help from any one. Do you understand that Cathy?"

"Well, the way you put it does sound right. I guess you are right. It's just been very upsetting for me, I couldn't think straight. I'm so glad you called Martin. I'll try to go see his parents and tell them what you'd like them to do."

"Thanks, very much, Cathy. This is very important to me. I'll explain more later in a letter and in the meantime I would appreciate hearing from you after you've talked with the Johnsons. Good-bye."

"Good-bye, Martin. Thanks again for calling. I feel much better after talking with you. Good-bye, you'll be hearing from me."

TWENTY-TWO

A Confession of Love

There was a flurry of activity as last minute preparations were made to leave San Francisco. Medical supplies were late arriving on the dock, and there were more stores to bring aboard. Periodically an enlisted man returning at the last minute from leave or liberty would come dashing aboard with a worn out excuse for his lateness. Among these was Scotty. The train was late, he told the O. D. But actually, he and Margaret had slept late on the Pullman, in their stateroom.

Margaret came along down to the dock because she wanted to see Martin before the ship sailed. They greeted one another with all the affection that can be shown between a brother and sister.

"It's good to see you again," Margaret said.

"Yes, it's good to see you too. I didn't expect to see you, but I'm glad you came along out here," Martin said.

"Well, taking our honeymoon on the train turned out just fine. We spent more time together that way. But I'm sure Mother and Dad are not too pleased with me."

As they talked a taxi pulled up near the gang plank where they were standing and out of it stepped a bedraggled young woman.

"Angela, it's Angela," Margaret screamed. "I don't believe it!" she said, still screaming. "How on earth did you get here?"

"It's a long story," Angela said, as she rushed into Martin's anxious arms. "When I heard that you and Scotty were taking your honeymoon on the train heading out here, I decided I would take off from work and try to make to here too before the guys leave. But I travelled by coach, and I saw the back yards of all the great American cities, New York, Erie, Cleveland, Chicago, Des Moines, Omaha, Cheyenne and all the rest in between. What a trip! But here I am, battered and worn, but happy to see you," she paused and smiled, "especially Martin." She hugged and kissed them all.

Lieutenant Rosetto saw the happy greeting from the bridge, and he rushed down to the main deck and then to the dock in record time. He greeted his sister warmly. "Angela, you're really something," he said. "I've never known you to get so serious about anyone as you are about Martin. I know you didn't come all the way out here to see me."

"Well, Frank, I'm happy to see you too," she said seriously, and she kissed him affectionately, almost passionately.

"What are we going to do?" Scotty asked. "We can't stand out here on the dock, and the ship is in an uproar getting ready to shove off."

"Maybe Lieutenant Rosetto would give us special permission to go ashore for lunch," Martin said boldly. "Could you arrange that for us, Lieutenant?"

"It just so happens that we have delayed departure time by four hours. The barge we are going to take in tow hasn't finished loading. We just got the word. So, O. K., you can go, but you must be back on board by 1500 hours."

"Oh, why don't you come along with us, Frank?" Angela pleaded. "I never get to spend any time with you."

"No, I'm sorry," Rosetto replied. "I still have too much to do to get ready. The four of you go have a nice lunch and be sure you get back here on time."

Angela gave her brother one last hug, and they headed for the street.

"I have reservations at the St. Francis Hotel," Margaret said. "I had planned to stay over one day before getting the train to go back home. Why don't we go there and freshen up and have lunch in the dining room?"

"That's a great idea," Angela said. "I don't have reservations, so maybe I could check in with you, Margaret. And I was hoping I would catch up with you and we could travel back together."

"Oh, certainly. You're more than welcome. I was dreading the thought of travelling alone after Scotty leaves."

By the time they reached the hotel they had decided the couples would take turns using Margaret's room, and while Angela and Martin were waiting for Scotty and Margaret, they had lunch in the dining room. As they sat there talking, Martin noticed that most of the other Navy men were officers, and he became aware again of the class differences between officers and enlisted men. Feelings of regret accompanied this awareness. Maybe enlisting as a seaman wasn't such a good idea after all. Oh, well, he thought, I only have six months more to go. Then he shrugged off those thoughts and paid attention to what Angela was saying.

"Travelling by coach on the train across the country, for a girl alone, is unbelievable," she said. "I was propositioned at least once every five hundred miles. I don't mean in any vulgar way, but I knew what those men's intentions were who tried to start up a conversation or acted so friendly and helpful. I'm beginning to wonder if that's all men think about when they see an unescorted woman."

This brought Martin's attention forcefully to another thought which had been bothering him since they made the plans to share the room. "Angela," he said, "I'm sorry, I feel like a heel for planning to go up to the room to make love with you. I haven't been faithful to you since we were together in New York, and I know I should have been."

"Oh, hush, Martin," Angela said. "Don't spoil our happy time together now. I'm not saying that I was unfaithful, but I know this much, we can't make one another such a promise, a promise to be faithful, not under these circumstances. I told you once before that I have known other sailors and I know that it is foolish to try to make such a promise when you are on sea-duty. We're not engaged. We can't even say we're going steady, not under the circumstances."

"Yeah, I remember now. It was when I called you in New York. I thought maybe you were saying good-bye for good. But what you were really saying is you don't want to tie yourself down, you don't want to go steady. Isn't that right?"

"What else, Martin? Do I have to spell out every word? Maybe I can't explain it exactly. I'm also saying that I don't want to obligate you. But nevertheless, the relationship, the attraction we have between us is something very special. You know that, don't you?"

"I sure do!" Martin said, remembering their night together in her parent's home, on the sofa and the floor. "I
know I'll always love you, Angela. It was really very nice
of you to travel all the way out here to see me." He looked
at his watch, becoming anxious now to go to the room.

"Well, maybe there was another reason I came out here.
I also wanted to see Frank again. Maybe I never really got
over being in love with Frank."

"With Frank, your brother?!"

"He's not really my brother, you know.   He was
adopted by my parents. I think I told you that. Martin,
will you promise not to tell anyone if I tell you a secret?"

"Sure," Martin answered, extremely curious now.

"Well, I loved Frank more than just as a brother. First I
had this teen-age crush on him. We grew up in the same
house as brother and sister and were always close. We
learned things together. But of course, we really weren't
related at all, except for the legal adoption. I found out
about the adoption from a cousin of mine who had heard
her parents discuss it.   Then when Frank was in the
academy we really fell in love, and when he was home one
Christmas, my mother caught us--in bed--and she told my
father, and, well it was just hell at home for a long time
afterwards. To keep peace in the family Frank promised
my parents he would break it up and never look at me
'that way' again. Those were some terrible days in our
lives. Frank probably got over it better than I did. He had
the academy and his Navy career. I was at home with my
parents, and they treated me like a criminal. They made
me feel guilty. They insisted that I regard Frank as a real
brother, some one you couldn't do 'anything like that'
with. But in truth, I was sincerely in love with a very at-

tractive man, and he was in love with me, and it wasn't easy to get over it."

"My God, that must have been horrible for you, for all of you," Martin mused.

"I've never told that to anyone, not even to Margaret, my best friend. So please don't ever tell Frank that I told you."

"I have no reason tell anyone," Martin reassured her.

"Which reminds me, by the way, Margaret told me all about Alice, your school sweetheart," said Angela. "She told me about your being engaged and that this Alice married someone else. She didn't volunteer the information. I grilled her until I got it out of her," she added smiling. "We're such good friends, she had to tell me. But she didn't seem to think that you were keeping that a secret. I just wanted you to know that I know."

"No, that's no secret," Martin said. Then he remembered that not even Margaret knew about Alice being pregnant. He hadn't told anyone about that. Should he tell Angela he wondered. But he decided not to tell her.

"Oh, look, here come Margaret and Scotty now," Angela said.

Scotty approached, snugly linked arm in arm with Margaret, displaying to all the world that they were lovers on their honeymoon. Martin and Angela lingered only a short time after they joined them at the table, finished their coffee, made small talk, and then went up to the room.

There was something totally different about Angela that Martin could not put into words. Their response to one another was still unique and indescribable. They relaxed as they gave one another mutual pleasure. But now Martin felt restricted. He felt like he was using someone else's personal property, like borrowing someone else's car; he couldn't do with it what he would if it were his own, he had to be careful with it, because it belonged to someone else. It was the same feeling he'd had with Jean Enderson. His relationship was now with a woman who belonged to another man, and only the fact that the time they had to spend together was limited kept him from acknowledging that their love affair was coming to an end.

Angela and Margaret went along back to the dock with them as he and Scotty returned on time. There seemed to be utter confusion up until the last minute as stragglers came dashing back aboard their ship amidst the bustle of last minute stowing by the shorthanded crew.

Frank Rosetto dashed down to the dock again and embraced Angela and bade her good-bye. He did not try to disguise the special affection he had for her, and Martin saw the look of pain on his face which revealed that theirs was a difficult parting. But at last the command, "Prepare to get underway," sounded over the ship's loudspeakers, and when the ships powerful diesel engines started Martin felt the vibrations underfoot, and these vibrations harmonized with the sounds coming from the engine room below.

"Cast off all lines," came the order from the Captain, who had taken the "conn" himself.

Martin and Scotty hauled in the stern line while other deck hands brought in the other lines. The powerful fleet tug moved slowly at first as it separated from the wharf, then smoothly picked up speed as it was maneuvered out into the placid waters of the San Francisco bay. Margaret and Angela stubbornly stayed on the dock and continued waving to them until they were out of sight.

They steamed past the commercial docks, and past Fisherman's Wharf. In the vicinity of the Naval Supply Depot, they took a large ammunition barge in tow and then continued. They passed Alcatraz Island and were soon passing under the Golden Gate Bridge again, and then onward, out to sea.

The Pacific Ocean, again, was all that its name implied, gigantic, boundless, pacific. Martin was thrilled at being a part of the force which was embodied by their powerful seagoing vessel, ploughing through this awesome body of water, with its huge steel barge, loaded with all types of Naval ammunition, firmly in tow.

"Our next port-of-call will be Pearl Harbor, Hawaii," the Captain announced, although everyone aboard already knew this through the grapevine. During the evening meal Martin sensed the excitement of his shipmates as they discussed shore leave or liberty in Honolulu, Waikiki Beach and other exotic places in the Hawaiian Islands, and shared their excitement.

After the evening meal Martin and Scotty walked out on the main deck and forward to the high point of the bow. From there they could see the great red glow into which they were heading, the setting sun, in the western sky. And Martin felt again that sense of loss, and the feeling of the present merging dialectically into the future of undreamed reality. But this time the horizon was aglow with the burning red fires of the promise of achievement, of fulfillment. He looked to the future with immense hope and excitement.

TWENTY-THREE

Calm Before the Storm

"I don't see why the hell we can't push up the speed of this old tub to fifteen knots and make it to Pearl by Saturday," said Lefty Flagner, the signalman, when Martin came up on the bridge to stand watch. Several of his shipmates had become disgruntled and complained bitterly when the Executive Officer changed the ETA, Pearl Harbor, from 1200, 6 December, to 0600, 7 December. They had anticipated going ashore in Honolulu on Saturday night. The new ETA meant there would be no liberty until Sunday.

The heavy steel barge, loaded as it was with ammunition, was at full draught, almost completely submerged in the seas, and towing it was more difficult than they had anticipated. Speed had even been reduced to six to eight knots for long stretches, and with the slower speed, the currents had carried them further north than estimated. Martin had discussed this with Lieutenant Rosetto as he went over their position and revised their course earlier that morning. Rosetto continued his daily instruction in the intricacies of navigation, for which Martin was grateful.

They steamed steadily for many days at the monotonous reduced speed, dragging their burdensome load behind them. Shipboard routine too was monotonous. Martin had duty on the bridge twice a day and the rest of the day he spent reading, eating, or sleeping. After about a week he had lost count of the days and he decided to take up his journal again which he had neglected since arriving in San Francisco. He recorded the correct date, 27 November, 1941. They had travelled seven days at a snail's pace, and their ETA, Pearl Harbor was 0600, 7 December, 1941. That meant nine more days. The weather was beautiful, he recorded, and getting warmer every day.

On the eighth night it was especially hot and stuffy below decks in the crew's quarters. Martin was very hot and restless. To escape the heat, which he assumed was the cause of his restlessness, Martin quietly took his mattress and went topside. He waved to the seaman on watch on the quarter deck and went aft to the fantail. There he unrolled his mattress on the large hatch cover on the starboard side, lay down on it and propped his head on his arms.

He lay there for a long time looking into a cloudy sky, seeing nothing, but listening to the steady beat of the ship's engines, which was superimposed on the rhythmic splashing as the fleet tug cut through the deep blue Pacific waters. Finally he drifted off into a troubled, turbulent sleep.

Hours later he woke up lying flat on his back. The sounds of the ship slicing through the placid water continued its rhythmic beat. But the skies now had cleared, and there was the clearest view of the heavens Martin had ever seen. As he studied it he became aware of the magnificence of the universe for the first time in his life. It was as if there were a million lights hanging overhead from invisible brackets and at different heights under a huge glass dome ceiling, and the most distant lights reached to infinity.

Martin remembered what he had learned about those countless stars in his astronomy course in college. The ones he could see, and the number was in the thousands, were part of a galaxy that was made up of billions of stars. And our galaxy, was only one of billions of galaxies in the universe. Incredible, absolutely incredible! He remembered at the time he studied this he had found it almost incomprehensible. Our sun, the sun we see rising every morning and setting every evening, is only one star of those billions and billions of stars in the universe; and the earth, which seems so solid, so secure, and so much the center of all things in existence, is by comparison only a small speck of clay, rock, water and air, rotating around that sun. And the moon, which at times seems so large, is only a small clump of minerals rotating around the earth, reflecting the sun's light, like a mirror. And, if the uncountable number of stars are suns like our own sun, then, he reasoned, there must be an infinite number of planets, like our own planet earth, rotating around those stars, and therefore, an infinite number of worlds like our own world, with the possibility of having on them living intelligent beings similar to ourselves.

This concept was, again, almost incomprehensible. But, there in the midst of the vast Pacific Ocean, floating on an infinitesimal speck of iron and steel, he himself an insignificant mass of living animal cells with a brain, for a fleeting moment he had a glimpse of eternity that was clear and intelligible. And, in that moment, it was as if all of the past, all of history, and all of the future were present and appeared as one huge still photograph, and all of the universe, and the earth's place in it could be clearly seen and understood. Time was not of the essence. There was no passing of hours or days or months, no years or centuries. It was all viewable now, in the present, clear, understandable, completely comprehensible, all in the brightness of that momentary flash of ultimate understanding.

To better analyze it, he tried to hold in view this clear thought, this moment of understanding, as you would hold a single frame of a motion picture film by stopping the projector. But fleeting it was, and it could not be held. Yet, in that fleeting moment, he grasped the truth which for so long had evaded him. This truth was the knowledge that there was something fundamentally wrong with the religion into which he had been born. The church teaching did not adequately describe God. The Genesis story of Adam and Eve, the concept of original sin, the Christmas story, the Easter story, all were inadequate to describe God and his relationship to man.

For in that moment of clear vision, it seemed to Martin that God is a vast, infinite, spiritually creative force which exists everywhere in the universe, without limit, with no beginning and with no end, a spiritually creative force that can not be described as a person. But in addition, he became aware of being a part of this creative force, as all mankind must be a part of it. This spiritually creative force was within him and he was in it. And it is this creative force which man personifies and names "God." To describe God as a father was totally inadequate. To describe God as a person, who is concerned with the details of our personal lives, now seemed egotistic and immature. It was not that the Bible or the catechism from which he had been taught were not honest attempts to teach truth and understanding. Rather, it was merely that they were inadequate.

Suddenly, after briefly assimilating this, he heaved a spontaneous sigh of relief. It was as if a huge burden had been lifted from his shoulders. Now he knew what had been the source of his discontent. He knew now why he had been unable to explain to his father, or to anyone else for that matter, why he chose not to go directly to the seminary, why he had instead joined the Navy. "Yes, yes, now I understand, now I see," he said aloud.

"What do you see?" a voice behind him asked. It was Lieutenant Rosetto. Martin was surprised. He had not noticed Rosetto's approach while he was absorbed in the elucidating thought processes through which he had just passed.

He hesitated momentarily to gather his thoughts. "From looking at this fantastically clear sky, I think I just drifted into some kind of a religious revelation," Martin answered. He tried to describe the visionary experience. He was still in awe of it. He could not formulate sentences to adequately translate it. But he described the experience to Rosetto with as much accuracy as he could summon and then concluded, "I started out just looking into the sky to identify some of the stars, planets and constellations I learned in the astronomy course I had at college, and that's where it led me."

"That's amazing," Rosetto said. "You were probably dreaming and dreamt part of something you may have read. That's the way dreams are. But on the other hand, you may have had a glimpse into the very depths of the 'one mind,' which Emerson described in his Essays--the one mind which is common to all history, and to all mankind. Have you read any of Ralph Waldo Emerson's essays? Now there is a man who really had some depth to his thinking."

"I tried reading Emerson several times and I know what you mean. But I didn't get very far. I found his essays to be heavy reading, difficult, but you do get a sense of there being more to human existence than what we can physically see."

"Well, that's the book I wanted to let you borrow. You should try it again. But speaking of astronomy," Rosetto said, deliberately changing the subject. "An astronomy course is an excellent background for learning navigation. I think you'll make a good navigator, and I want to talk to you about that, later. But I was looking for you just then, Martin, because I have something else to discuss with you," Rosetto said, with a changed look of seriousness.

"Yes, Sir," Martin answered, catching the changed mood. "What is it, Sir?"

"I hate to say it, but it's the Jim Johnson thing again. We received a message from the Judge Adjutant General's Office. You are to be held for a General Court Martial for the murder of Jim Johnson. You are to be held until we are notified where the General Court Martial will be convened, which I assume will be at Pearl Harbor. I'm sorry, Martin."

"Jesus," Martin said under his breath. "I was afraid this would happen. Must you put me in the brig?"

"No, I've discussed it with the Captain. You will be a prisoner-at-large on this ship until we get orders for your transfer."

"Lieutenant, if they give me a General Court Martial, will you be my Navy defense counselor?"

"I was hoping you would ask. I'll be happy to defend you, because I don't think you killed Johnson. But, only the Captain and I, and you, know about this. Even though the message was taken by the radioman, it was in code, and I decoded it myself. So, do not tell anyone about this, until we know more about it. We don't want any unnecessary scuttlebutt aboard the ship. Understand?"

"Yes, Sir, and thank you, Lieutenant," Martin answered, as he turned to walk away.

TWENTY-FOUR

December 7th at Pearl Harbor

Sunday morning, 7 December, Martin crawled out of his bunk earlier than usual. He knew that wind drift and currents had taken the ship further north again. They would be coming in high in the Kaiwi Channel between Molokai and Oahu. They would not be able to see Molokai, but they would have a close up view of Koko Head Point on Oahu, and the famous Diamond Head.

Martin had found a convenient spot for observation when he was off duty, on the starboard side, just aft of the whale boat davit (lifeboat). It was a protected area, hidden from sight of the bridge. He had spent many hours there whenever there was anything to observe from the starboard side, or just to sit and think and watch the passing sea. He could sit there or stand, and there were plenty of brackets and braces to hang on to if the seas got rough.

As he climbed into his hideaway that morning before breakfast, the crow's nest lookout shouted loudly to the bridge, "Lights ahead off starboard bow." Martin leaned outboard for a better look and saw the lights off in the distance, and assumed that they were from Koko Head. Then, just as the sun was rising, Diamond Head came clearly into view, and shortly thereafter, Honolulu.

Later as they approached the Pearl Harbor Channel entrance, a four-stacker destroyer was sighted some distance up ahead. It was firing some of its guns and apparently dropping depth charges. Martin crossed over to the port side to get a better look, but it was still too far distant to determine exactly what the destroyer was doing. He was to learn later that when the Captain reported their arrival to the Commandant, 14th Naval District, he was instructed to move into Pearl Harbor at once. "We have reports of an unidentified submarine operating in vicinity of channel entrance. Report any craft sightings immediately," the message ordered.

Martin rushed through breakfast and dashed into the crew's head, as he always did, for last minute relief before going on watch. He had the 0800 to 1200 watch, but he liked to get to the bridge about ten minutes early to look over the navigator's charts and chat with the quartermaster before relieving the watch. As he passed through the mess hall, on the way to the bridge, a local, commercial radio station was giving the weather report: "Mostly clear today, with some clouds in the mountains."

When he got to the bridge, Lieutenant Rosetto was at the navigator's board going over the charts and maps. After acknowledging Martin's presence, he said, "Our radioman intercepted a message from the USS WARD stating they had attacked and dropped depth charges on an unidentified submarine."

The Captain had taken the "conn" himself in view of the situation, and probably would have regardless of the situation, because he would not trust anyone else to take his ship and its tow into this complex naval operations center. Neither he nor any of his officers had ever been here before. He had requested a harbor pilot, but due to the circumstances, he was to proceed through the channel immediately.

With the Captain at the "conn," they steamed into the channel, maneuvering through the submarine nets which had been opened to allow them to go through. Captain Mills was using excessively high speed, something he seldom did with a heavy load in tow. Excitement permeated the bridge. The Captain got on the loudspeakers and announced: "All hands, now hear this. We are now entering Pearl Harbor Channel. All hands be prepared . . ."

The rest of his message was left unspoken, for without warning, the sky was suddenly filled with the loud droning sounds of many airplanes.

Martin had just reached the bridge when he heard the terrible droning overhead, and it seemed to him that the biblical prophesy had finally come to pass. The destruction of the earth had commenced. For he saw up ahead tremendous black, heavy smoke rising high into the sky. Rumbling and explosions could be heard. Fire and smoke were shooting up everywhere. Utter confusion broke out on the bridge, and this was amplified because there were double the number of men on the bridge during the changing of the watch. But complete order and calm soon were restored by the sobering realization of what was happening. Pearl Harbor was under attack from the sky! Airplanes, bombers, dive bombers and fighter planes were attacking the United States Pacific Fleet in the harbor as well as the shore installations.

The Captain's leadership ability was immediately apparent. For in just a few minutes, he was in complete control of the entire ship. First he sounded the general alarm. Then he grabbed the loudspeaker microphone from the talker, and ordered: "All hands man your battle stations. This is the real thing. Pearl Harbor is under attack by Japanese military forces."

This command immediately cleared the bridge of any extra personnel, as every man dashed for his battle station. Martin's battle station was the very same duty of Captain's Talker for which he had been trained and for which he had just reported for duty when he relieved the watch. He took the earphones headset from the man he was relieving, put them on and then placed the special steel helmet over them.

Then he checked out the sound-powered phones by calling out, "Division officers report when ready," as he had been trained to do.

There was immediate response: "Gunnery Officer here. All gunners on station and ready."

"Gunnery officer reports all gunners on station and ready, Captain," Martin repeated. One of the gunners is Scotty, thought Martin. Scotty is on one of the twenty millimeter antiaircraft guns they had on the wings of the bridge on each side of the ship. It was reassuring to have those guns for the self-defense of their ship, he thought, as well as the two forty millimeter antiaircraft guns mounted in turrets, and the one three inch mounted up on the forecastle.

Then, the message, "This is the Damage Control Officer. Damage control crew standing by and ready."

"Damage control standing by and ready," Martin repeated.

"Aye, aye," the Captain acknowledged.

The same type of message followed from the Firefighting division and from the engine room. When all battle stations were manned, the Captain radioed Com14, Operations, in code:

"WE HAVE HEAVY AMMUNITION BARGE IN TOW. NOW INSIDE SUBMARINE NETS IN PEARL CHANNEL. PRESENT ORDERS ARE TO REPORT TO NAVY YARD. DUE CIRCUMSTANCES, WE AWAIT FURTHER ORDERS."

It seemed like they'd waited forever for an answer. In the meantime, they continued steaming up the channel at about eight knots. Growing impatient, the Captain, at one point shouted, "God damn it. What the hell are they waiting for? Don't they know we could block the whole god damn channel if this barge gets hit?" He wasn't talking to anyone in particular.

Meanwhile the holocaust continued all over Pearl Harbor, over all of it they could see, at least. Martin saw the tremendous explosions and huge bellows of thick, black smoke rising everywhere on the starboard side, which he viewed through one of the portholes on the bridge. He thought of all the men on all those ships and on the docks and on the airfields. Hundreds must be dead or dying. "Good God! I don't believe what's happening here," he muttered to himself. "My God, we're not even at war with the Japanese."

But, finally, Operations Control came through, uncoded:

"GET THAT THING OUT OF THE CHANNEL AT FULL SPEED. PROCEED TO EAST LOCH AT ONCE. STAY WEST OF FORD ISLAND. ANCHOR BARGE IN CLEAR AREA. THEN GIVE FULL ASSISTANCE TO USS UTAH."

Captain Mills fired off an acknowledgment of the orders and then gave the command: "FULL SPEED AHEAD." They proceeded up the channel at 15 knots, with Waipio Peninsula off to port. Then soon he spotted Hospital Point on Keanapuaa on the starboard side. Bombs were falling and torpedoes exploding all over the harbor, but they were still a safe distance away.

Their progress was agonizingly slow, even at fifteen knots. But they could not go faster. The deck officer reported maximum stress on the main tow line and winch.

Martin was keenly alert and extremely tense as he attempted to stay aware of everything that was taking place. He was eager to relay each and every one of the Captain's orders and the responses with accuracy and dispatch. Presently, they were in view of Ford Island, which was a mass inferno, and to the east of it they could see the long line of battle ships and cruisers, which Martin was to learn was called Battleship Row.

It was a sickening sight, the damaged, burning, capsized ships, the flames, the smoke, the explosions, the utter chaos. The entire proud, American Pacific Naval Force, mercilessly battered, on its knees, apparently helpless and hardly able to retaliate.

The personnel on the bridge became strangely silent as they proceeded at their slow but steady pace. Only an occasional outburst of disbelief, in hushed tones, from the Captain or some other individual could be heard:

"Good damn!"

"Son-of-a-bitch."

"Holy shit."

"Holy hell."

"Jesus Christ, look at that!"

There were high-level bombers overhead and dive bombers launching torpedoes, and fighters strafing anything in sight. Although it was all taking place at quite some distance away, it appeared that Ford Island, the Navy Yard and ships in the Southeast Loch were getting the brunt of the savage onslaught.

Then, abruptly, the bombing and strafing stopped, and the planes disappeared in the sky. Behind them, the anti-aircraft batteries from ashore and afloat also stopped. Only the burning ships and buildings, the explosions, and the black smoke continued. The whole scene became momentarily quiet, except for an occasional internal explosion from one or another of the burning ships.

By the time they reached the UTAH, the great battleship had capsized and was bottom up and barely visible. There were numerous small craft all around picking up the few remaining survivors who were still in the water. Captain Mills surveyed the situation and then radioed the message to Operations:

"UTAH BEYOND OUR HELP. PROCEEDING TO EAST LOCH WITH BARGE. AWAITING FURTHER ORDERS."

Martin borrowed a set of binoculars from Lieutenant Rosetto and panned the entire Pearl Harbor area. The sight was incredible! He had never seen such a concentration of Naval power. How could he have known that such a massive force ever existed? But, now, there it was in front of his own eyes, a twisted, helpless mass of useless iron and steel in smoking ruins. Surely, the end of the world had come.

But the powerful fleet tug, with its own burden of potential destruction firmly in tow, continued on its course.

They swung wide around the UTAH and proceeded steadily toward their destination, the clear area in the middle of East Loch. They would not be able to render any assistance to any ships until they were relieved of the barge. Finally they reached the designated area, and they pulled the barge into position. The main tow line was disconnected and reeled in. Then they pulled up alongside where deck hands boarded the barge and dropped its anchors.

At last they were free and then awaited anxiously their next orders from Operations. The message arrived:

"GIVE FIRE FIGHTING AND FULL ASSISTANCE TO THE NEVADA."

TWENTY-FIVE

A Hell of a Mess

The USS NEVADA was at the end of Battleship Row, off of the northeast point of Ford Island. Captain Mills headed the FLEET TUG toward the NEVADA immediately. "Full speed ahead," he ordered, and Martin could feel the unburdened floating powerhouse leap forward like a large, fierce dog breaking its restraining chain. The battleship was burning violently, and smoking profusely, but it was getting underway nevertheless. It was headed toward the channel and apparently via the west side of Ford Island.

"Firefighting Officer make ready all firefighting equipment to give all out assistance to the Nevada," the Captain ordered.

"Firefighting reports all equipment ready, Captain," Martin relayed.

"Aye, aye," Captain Mills acknowledged.

Soon they were alongside the huge, flaming battleship. Captain Mills attempted to make contact with it via the ship-to-ship telephone. The damaged NEVADA had not yet responded when suddenly the sky was filled again with the awful droning of many airplanes. And in a few minutes the dive bombers started diving in and launching their torpedoes again, and the high-level bombers unleashed their bombs again. Fighters made more strafing runs. The already crippled ships were apparently prime targets for this second onslaught, as well as the ships that had not been hit by the first of the savage raiders.

This time, however, there were more antiaircraft batteries in action. More men were in place manning their guns now than there were during the first sneak attack, which had come without warning. Dogfights by a few undamaged American fighter planes could be seen and heard. The whole harbor and the air bases were again under attack. The smoke and the flames increased again and the sky was filled with the flak of antiaircraft tracer bullets from the ships and shore installations.

Martin saw dive bombers coming at the flaming NEVADA, coming in low and close, dropping their bombs and strafing. The NEVADA's guns came to life with a deafening roar, and the FLEET TUG's own anti-aircraft guns commenced firing on the Captain's order, "All gunners fire at will on attacking aircraft." But even while he was saying this, out of the confusion, a dive bomber was coming at the NEVADA on their side. Martin saw Scotty fire on it with his 20 millimeter, and miraculously, he got it with a direct hit. The pilot was able to drop his bombs, but they were near misses, alongside the NEVADA.

Unfortunately, the pilot also, somehow, managed to return Scotty's fire with machine gun bullets. Watching through the open compartment door of the bridge, Martin saw the most horrifying sight imaginable. Machine gun bullets riddled Scotty's body, and his face suddenly disappeared in a blob of blood. His body jerked momentarily as if he were being electrocuted, then he slumped to the deck in a formless heap. It all happened in a few seconds. The Japanese bomber, though smoking and burning, pulled out of his dive and climbed upward and was temporarily out of sight.

Martin acted out of sheer instinct and fright. He pulled off his sound-powered headset and helmet, and dashed out on to the wing of the bridge. He picked up Scotty and cradled him in his arms like a child, but it was like picking up a quarter of a beef or a freshly slaughtered calf -- a lifeless, 150 pounds of warm bloodied flesh. He spoke for Scotty and for all the ship's officers and men as he rushed with him in his arms toward the sick bay, shouting at the top of his voice, "You lousy sons-a-bitches. You lousy bastards. We'll get you for this. We'll get you for this, you lousy no good, goddamn bastards." They were Scotty's words, the way Scotty would have said them, and that is all he could do for his brother-in-law and good friend. But Scotty could not appreciate the challenging words uttered on his behalf, for he was dead!

When he got to the sick bay he laid the lifeless, formless heap of bleeding flesh on the examining table, and was overwhelmed with sickening grief. The Pharmacist's Mate took hold of his arm and led him out of the sick bay. But he could indulge in grief only a few short minutes, for as he was responding to the Captain's voice on the loudspeaker, "Miller, return to your battle station at once," he could hear the roar of the crippled dive bomber. It was deliberately headed for a crash dive on the NEVADA. But then suddenly, as if he decided he couldn't make it to the battleship, or perhaps out of a last second desire for revenge on the gun that had downed him, the pilot veered his plane toward the FLEET TUG and deliberately crashed it into the bridge. The ripping, tearing, exploding sounds were sickening, horrifying. The horrendous impact and the explosions caused multiple concussions which seemed to Martin to be jarring his head loose from the inside out. The resulting concussion threw him back down the ladder to the second deck from which he had just climbed. When he reached bottom he struck the back of his head a resounding blow, and he momentarily blacked out. But he did not completely lose consciousness. Blood began to run down the back of his neck from the cut in his scalp.

He picked himself up as quickly as he was able and shook off the feeling of slipping into unconsciousness. He scurried back up the ladder. But instead of climbing the ladder to the bridge from the inside, Martin stepped out on the main deck. He looked up to where the bridge had been. The sight was beyond belief. It had all but disappeared. Where are the men? he thought, as he climbed the outside ladder to the bridge deck. The rear bulkhead was bent and twisted, although still standing, but the rest of what had been the bridge was a mass of twisted steel. Behind the ship's superstructure the mainmast had been sheared off. But intermingled with the twisted mass of wires and steel were the scattered parts of the men who had been on duty on the bridge. He should have been there with them. It was his battle station. God! Scotty's death had given him his life! He climbed around in the wreckage, searching franticly. The Captain, there, parts of him, and Lefty Flagner, the signalman. He stepped on and then slipped off of a bloody steel girder and fell into another space where, in horror, he saw Frank Rosetto. That was it! He could stand no more! He was beginning to get sick to his stomach when Chief McCroye grabbed him by the arm and said, "Martin, come along now, get the hell out of here. Come to the sick bay, before you bleed to death. Damage Control can handle things here." Mc-Croy's damage control party was up in the bridge area and had started the job of removing the bodies and assessing the damage.

"No, no!" Martin shouted. "I've got Lieutenant Rosetto here and I think he's alive. Give me a hand here, quick." As he said this he spit out the sour stomach fluid that had surfaced into his mouth. McCroy responded instinctively and beckoned one of the other crewmen.

They pulled Frank Rosetto out from under the battered steel. They put him on a stretcher and took him immediately to the sick bay. There Martin saw that Mathews, the Pharmacist's Mate, had already put Scotty's body into a canvas bag.

"Take that back on the fantail," he said, pointing to Scotty's canvas bag. "And put the Exec. on the table."

Rosetto had regained consciousness and was muttering something about the ship's log, but no one was paying any attention to what he was saying, except Martin. He understood, and he quickly dashed back up to the bridge and searched through the area where the ship's log had been kept. He found it in the steel cabinet drawer, still intact, where it was always kept when there were no entries being made in it. He rushed back down to the sick bay and placed the log into Rosetto's hands.

"How is he?" Martin asked Mathews, the Pharmacist.

"He doesn't appear to have any broken bones, but he must really be hurting with internal injuries. I gave him a shot of morphine. But we've got to get him to a hospital. He's got cuts and bruises all over him." The Pharmacist's Mate looked at Martin, as if critically examining him, and then asked, "How are you doing?"

"O. K., I guess," Martin answered and he suddenly became aware of his own pain, especially the pain inside his head. "I could use some aspirin, maybe," he said.

"Let me have a look at your head," Mathews said. He looked into Martin's eyes and then examined the wound on the back of his head. "The blood's congealed and the bleeding has stopped, but you need some stitches there. It's a pretty big cut you got there."

Then he turned his attention to one of the fire fighting crewman being brought into the sick bay. He was badly injured. "This sick bay isn't big enough for more than one patient at a time," Mathews said. "Will you move Scott Ackermun now, please."

Martin and one of the damage control crewman picked up the canvas bag and struggled up the ladder with it to the main deck. Back on the fantail, four other bags were lined up on top of the large hatch cover. Two of the bags were only partially filled. One of them was Captain Mills.

As Martin was returning toward the bow, a motor launch pulled up alongside. It was from the hospital ship SOLACE which was anchored nearby in East Loch. A Chief Pharmacist's Mate and two seaman came aboard. They conferred with Mathews and Lieutenant Rosetto who was now automatically the ship's commanding officer.

While they conferred the USS NEVADA steamed away defiantly, under its own power, headed for the channel. It was still in flames, but fighting its own fires and apparently had them under control.

The Chief Pharmacist's Mate from the SOLACE agreed to take all of the FLEET TUG's dead and the severely injured. There were five dead: Captain Harry B. Mills, Ensign Bruce Bradley, the ship's communications officer, Signalman Lawrence (Lefty) Flagner, Chief Quartermaster Charles Bartholemew, and Seaman Scott Ackermun. And there were seven badly injured, including Lieutenant Frank Rosetto.

Martin leaned against the rail to steady himself, and Mathews looked at him and said: "Maybe you should go along, Miller, you need repairs to your head."

To which Martin muttered to himself, "Yeah, I need repairs on my head, both outside and inside." He was beginning to see black spots before his eyes. He had difficulty trying to remember what they were doing and why. He looked at Rosetto, who appeared to be slipping into unconsciousness or sleep, lying there on a stretcher, still clutching the ship's log. Martin stared for a long time at the log and wondered why Rosetto was so concerned about it at a time like this. He glared at the canvas bags stacked on the launch and his stomach began to heave again; then his eyes panned out over the utter destruction of Pearl Harbor again, with its veil of black smoke, its drowning, its screaming injured, its dying and its dead. He bit down hard on his lips to keep them from quivering and to keep from shouting at the top of his voice; but he could not contain it.

"Oh, my God! And I wanted to be a minister! I wanted to teach others about the brotherhood of man. I wanted to teach others about a personal, loving God. I had some doubts, but look at this! How can I ever teach that now? Look what they've done to us. Look what they've done to all those people. Look what they've done to the mighty U. S. Navy. Look what has been done to the United States of America. Would a loving, caring, omnipotent God allow this to happen to his children? If this is some kind of punishment for America, the work of a vengeful God, then I want nothing more to do with such a God. Mathews, I don't have to go to the Hospital ship," he said, defiantly. "Just give me a couple of stitches and some aspirin." He placed his hand on the back of his head to feel the wound. "It isn't that bad. Give me a hand with Rosetto."

"O. K." Mathews said, as he grabbed one end of Rosetto's stretcher.

But just as they were lowering Rosetto over the side to the launch, he became fully conscious again. He looked around in bewilderment.

"What the hell's going on here?" he yelled.

"We're taking you to the SOLACE to see a doctor," the SOLACE's Chief Pharmacist's Mate told him.

"Hell, no, you're not," Rosetto roared. "I'm the Commanding Officer of this ship. Captain Mills is dead. Put me back up there on deck."

"Yes, Sir," the Chief responded, apparently not inclined to argue with the officer in command. "We've got more casualties than we can possibly handle, just look out there." They put him back up on deck. Then the SOLACE personnel jumped into their launch and roared away.

Rosetto stood up, trying to conceal the pain. He surveyed the situation. "Martin, get the Damage Control Officer and Chief McCroye and then come with me."

"Yes, Sir," Martin answered, rushed away, but quickly returned with Ensign Henry Freeda, and Chief McCroye.

As they climbed the ladder to the bridge, Lieutenant Rosetto yelled back down to Lt. William Kinser, the Engineering Officer, "Check out all gear for activating the helm amidships, and prepare to get underway, we are drifting too close to the other crippled ships."

"Aye, aye, Sir," Kinser responded.

TWENTY-SIX

Resolution and Hope

Lieutenant Rosetto, who had now taken command of the ship, ordered that the "con" be set up temporarily on the forecastle.

"Martin, I want you to take over the communications officer's duties," Rosetto ordered. Have intercom phones set up and connected at the helm amidships, we'll steer from there, and we'll set up a temporary chart room in the wardroom."

After Lt. Kinser, the Engineering Officer, reported all engines and propulsion gear, and the helm ready to get underway, Rosetto ordered, "Half speed forward, easy right rudder, steady as you go," as he maneuvered the FLEET TUG back into East Loch. "We should be safe here temporarily," Rosetto said. After they anchored and shut down the engines, he called all officers and Chief Petty Officers to a meeting in the wardroom. He asked Martin to join them.

"First, I want to announce that I have assigned Martin Miller as the ship's Communications Officer, as a temporary assignment. He will also assist me as navigator, if we go to sea. Even though Miller is only a Seaman Second Class, he is a college graduate in civilian life and he is the best qualified and available for this assignment at the present time. I plan to get him a field commission as an officer as soon as we can communicate with the Commandant of the 14th Naval District. "Unfortunately, our Radioman, Jeff Masters is one of the severely injured who are on the SOLACE. Also, as is fairly obvious, our radio transmitter is badly damaged and the antenna completely destroyed. Also our signal lights were destroyed along with the superstructure and mainmast. So, even though our engines, our main propulsion and everything below decks is in good order, and we can steer from amidships, we are, you might say, dead in the water. We can't get very far until we can get the radios fixed and new visual equipment.

"Because of this situation, and because I need a couple of days to do a little healing, Lieutenant Kinser, I am asking you to take the whale boat and go ashore to the Commandant's Office, as my personal representative and report our situation. We were supposed to be assigned to a Task Force of the Pacific Fleet, but I suppose that is all out of the picture under the circumstances. With all those damaged ships out there, there's no way of knowing what our next orders will be.

"All of you officers and Chiefs pass the word to all hands. I don't feel up to a speech at General Quarters, but we want to try to keep up the morale of the crew by keeping our plans and intentions posted. Incidentally, Martin Miller will be eating with the officers mess, replacing Ensign Bradley, and he should be extended all the courtesies of an officer. It is time for the noon meal now, but I am going to excuse myself and get some much needed rest."

Rosetto left the wardroom and the mess boys served up the noon meal. Martin felt somewhat intimidated, sitting there in his seaman's dungarees, eating with the officers. It was an abrupt change from eating in the enlisted men's mess hall, and when he thought of the fact that his usual mealtime companion, Scotty, no longer existed he almost lost his appetite. But, life goes on, he thought, for the living, and an individual must learn to cope with whatever life has to offer, and go on living. Although each of them congratulated him on his swift promotion, the conversation seemed equally as awkward for all of the other officers as well. But with three officers missing from the mess, Captain Mills, Ensign Bradely and Rosetto up in his cabin, there were only three others present beside himself, and after considering this, Martin realized why Lieutenant Rosetto had acted so swiftly in appointing him a temporary officer. While they ate, officers and enlisted men's battle stations and watches were reassigned to adjust for the reduction in the number of officers and men. Martin got the 1200 to 1600 Officer of the Deck duty, which was an ordeal, getting accustomed to the officer role in the presence of his former enlisted friends. It would take him, and them, some time to adjust to the new relationship, he thought.

When he was relieved of the watch, at 1600 hours, a message from Rosetto was delivered to him by messenger, to report to the Rosetto's cabin.

"I wanted to talk to you about a serious matter," Rosetto said immediately as Martin entered the cabin. "I seem to sense that you are having some reservations about being an officer, and I've been thinking about that outburst you had awhile ago down on the main deck, and about some of the conversations we've had concerning your struggle with your beliefs and your indecision about going into the ministry."

"Yes, Lieutenant, I'm really embarrassed by that out-burst. I guess the circumstances, the conditions at that moment were, I'd say, overwhelming. I was beside myself with anger and, and vengeance. I guess I shot off my mouth unconsciously, out of anger. Actually, in my own mind I have already retracted my statement about rejecting God. Even if everything that organized religion has de-vised to attempt to describe God's existence is inadequate, I think most human beings know that a supreme being of some kind exists. It seems to be an innate knowledge, and I cannot reject God even if I don't understand how this un-godly mess was allowed to happen."

"You may be right, Martin. It has occurred to me that you and I have much in common, even though I'm a num-ber of years older than you. You started out and were well on your way to making a career in the ministry. I made the Navy my career as an officer. I know that you were, or still are, going through a period of trying to decide whether you want to buckle down and accept all that is necessary to make a life's commitment to the ministry. That's why you have had all the doubts and the questions about your beliefs. I had somewhat the same kind of pe-riod after I graduated from the Naval Academy. One of the things that really bothered me was that I had to accept as gospel all those old Navy customs and traditions and rules and regulations.

"One of my old professors at the academy, used to take great pride in quoting from 'A Retired Admiral to his Son,' which were published letters written by a Captain A. P. Niblach, back in 1913. I don't know them all, word for word, but, as best as I can remember one of them goes something like: Does it pay to be a naval officer? That depends on whether you are prepared to play the game. Obedience to the law is liberty. If you keep the law, it pays. If you're always trying to prove you have the courage of your convictions, it may not pay. If you play the game, if you put nothing ahead of your profession, if you pocket your opinions, it pays. Otherwise it may not.'"

"That was tough advice for me to take, and I can see you are having the same problem with it I had," Rosetto said.

"You're right," said Martin, "that would be hard advice for me to take even from my own father."

"But it was the rest of that letter that's more convincing," Rosetto said. "He told his son that the naval profession is almost like the ministry. You dedicate your life to a purpose. You wear the clothes of an organized profession. You live your life by the rules of the organization. You renounce the pursuit of wealth. You practically give up your citizenship and you stay out of politics. You work for the highest good of the organization. Your goals are as moral as any ministers, because morality is looking after the best interests of civilization. You are not just seeking your own good, but working for the good of your country! You help to teach the men under you morality, and just like a minister, what you say must be in accordance the rules laid down by your organization. So, you see what I mean, we have this problem in common. So much of the old Navy rules and regulations, the customs and traditions are so outdated, or as you say of your religious beliefs, no longer relevant, and yet, if we want to be a part of these professions, we have to accept what's already established within them. We have to accept, conform, and 'play the game.'"

"Yes," Martin said. "I see what you mean, and I guess I've had a real struggle with that concerning the organized church."

"But, look, Martin," Rosetto said, intensely absorbed in the subject now, "if I may give you just a little of my personal philosophy. The laws for the conduct of human society, when entrusted to interpretation by human beings, and who else is there, can be misinterpreted and must be continuously reviewed and re-examined to insure that they are applicable to the times to which they are applied, and not to situations which are no longer relevant. Religious and moral laws, civil as well as military and naval laws are similar to physical laws. We cannot treat modern diseases, which have developed in modern times, with old remedies for diseases which no longer exist. Human nature and the environment in which we humans live are constantly changing. These changes are subtle and evolve slowly. Religious, moral, civil, as well as military and naval laws must therefore be changed accordingly, and it is the professionals within these fields who must recognize these subtle changes and take the necessary action to keep up with them."

"So, let me ask you this, Martin. Where can you serve best to help make the changes you believe are needed in your religion? Inside the church or outside? In the religion into which you were born you have the best example of how this should be handled. Ask yourself, what would Martin Luther have done in this situation? Remember, when he found intolerable practices, abuses of authority, and precepts which he could not accept, he posted his 95 theses on the church door, or wherever it was, and he stood his ground. As a Naval officer or as a minister, we can do that too. I believe old Captain Niblack; we have to accept, conform and play the game, most of the time, but I also believe there are times when we must take a stand and work for the necessary changes. And you can do it if you believe strongly enough in what you think needs changing, and you have the guts to do it, but only if you are part of the organization, not outside of it."

"I understand what you are saying," said Martin, "and I think this is helping me clear up some conflicts in my mind. But what happened here this morning is turning everything upside down. We'll all have to do some rethinking about a whole raft of things."

"Yes, you're right, a lot of what I said is for the future. Looking around us, at this moment, we can see, from what the Japanese have done to us here, that we have an extremely serious, powerful and treacherous enemy. Who knows if and at what moment those bastards will hit us again. God forbid, not now! At this moment we are at the bottom of a pit. I have no doubt that somehow we, Americans, will survive this mess and we'll have our revenge. But from what we can see now, it looks like it may be a long, arduous fight. Nothing, nothing, will ever be the same again for any of us. Nothing in our country can ever be the same after this defeat. Nothing in the world will ever be the same, and nothing in the Navy will ever be the same. And that creates opportunities in the Navy for many of us. I expect to be the Commanding Officer of a ship from now on until I retire or die, and that's why I am offering you a field commission. I know you are officer material and I'll need an Executive Officer. You'll have to serve in the military now, one way or another. So will you accept the commission and work with me for the next couple of years?"

Martin had listened carefully and with great interest to what Rosetto was saying, and as was his manner, he thought it over carefully before answering. "That sounds very interesting for the present," he said, "and I'm ready to say, Yes sir, except for my one big, immediate problem. Remember? There's the court-martial I am to face here."

"Oh, of course, Martin, I was well aware of that," Rosetto said, smiling, as he reached over on his desk, picked up the ship's log and pulled out a typed radio message. "That's one reason I know you are officer material. The action that you took on your own behalf, by getting Jim Johnson's parents, through Cathy Welsh, to insist on an autopsy on Johnson, and by getting me to intercede with my friends in Norfolk, that worked. An autopsy was made, and it showed conclusively that Johnson died of a massive heart attack. He would have died regardless, and if his medical records hadn't been mishandled, he would have been out of the Navy on a medical discharge a long time ago. The order to place you under arrest and hold you for trial by general court-martial has been rescinded. This typed radio message explains it all. I received it from the radioman just before we were hit by that Jap plane, and I stuck it into the ship's log. I was going to tell you when you came on watch, but then . . . well you know the rest. Congratulations," Rosetto said, as he shook Martin's hand.

"Wow," Martin responded. "So much is happening so fast. What a relief!" He tried, but he could not stop the tears from rolling down his cheeks. He turned his head aside and quickly brushed them away.

Rosetto put his arm around Martin's shoulder, and embraced him as he would a brother. "That's over and done with now, Martin," he said. "But, we have a long, hazardous journey ahead of us. Let's turn our attention and our energies to the task at hand."

"Aye, aye, Sir," Martin said, brightening up and smiling. "I thank you for the faith and confidence you have shown in me. I'm grateful for the good opinion you have of me, and I'm sure you know that the feeling is mutual. I'll excuse myself now and let you get some rest. Good night, . . Captain."

"Good night," Rosetto said, smiling. "And if you write to Angela, tell her I asked about her. I just can't get myself to write a letter."

"Frank," Martin said. "For Angela's sake, and your own, why don't you write her a letter. She's still in love with you." Then Martin turned and left immediately. He didn't want to hear Rosetto's answer. He went directly to the ward room and wrote the letter he had himself put off for too long. It was as follows:

December 7, 1941

Dearest Alice,
    By the time you receive this letter you will have heard what happened this morning in Hawaii. My ship arrived at Pearl Harbor only a short time before the Japanese attacked. No words can describe the horror that took place here and I won't try to give a full account. The picture of this unbelievable event has been etched into my memory as an indelible picture of hell, fire and damnation. My ship was hit and brutally damaged, but not

sunk. Five of our ship's officers and men are dead, including the Captain and my good friend, Scott Ackermun.

I don't know what this all means in terms of God's existence, or God's influence in the life of man. What I see now is what Hobbes said long ago of man's existence, ". . . and worst of all, continual fear, and danger or violent death; and the life of man, solitary, poor, brutish and short." What I see all around me here is a frightening example of the immorality and the inhumanity of man. The Japanese have just demonstrated the natural animal nature of man, unbridled, uninhibited and free of any religious or moral restraints. With the dead and the dying and the destruction all around us here I can see now, and appreciate, the enormity of the problem, the task that is faced by organized religion. Considering the nature of man, morality, civilized behavior and even humanity, may be artificial elements that must be superimposed upon and instilled in people; and that task has only just begun. The efforts of our religious and moral institutions may not be adequate to the task. But what else do we have? What else or who else is dedicated to such a goal? Misguided and inadequate though they may be, they are all that we have. They are our only hope for continuing to build a civilized world, and we must start from where we are and work with what we have.

This shocking and infamous tragedy here at Pearl Harbor, has abruptly thrust upon me a clear awareness of the responsibility that is my fate, and makes clear, once and for all, that my 'calling' is to the ministry. For the near future it looks as if I'll have to stay in the Navy and help to try to restore our country to its rightful place in the world. I'm sure all of us agree that we can't let the Japanese destroy our American institutions and all the good that has been established in our country. But when this has been accomplished and I can go back home again, I would like to go home to my wife and my child--I mean you, Alice, and our child. You may or may not have noticed that I've never really expressed my opinion of your decision to go along with Charles Smith's suggestion that the two of you just raise our child as if Charles were the father. I have no doubts whatsoever, now, that I cannot agree to such an arrangement. If you can still love me just as much as you love Charles, I think we should both make every effort to get together as soon as possible.

I have never stopped loving you, Alice. You just went ahead and did what you wanted to do. But, of course, so did I, and I realize that I am to blame for causing the big change in the direction of our lives. But I have never stopped loving you. And, though at first I did nothing, or rather was not in a position to do anything, about what you did, I am now, with this letter, asking you to get a divorce, go back home to Pennsylvania, have our baby and look after our child until the day that I can come home to our wedding. This may be asking a lot of you, Alice. I know this. But I think it is what will be right for the three of us. Please consider this seriously, and then do it. We both allowed ourselves to be side-tracked. Hopefully each of us has learned from these experiences. But now it is time to get back on the main track again and put our lives back together, where we belong. Heaven only knows how long it will be until we can be together again, but in the meantime, let's keep up a steady correspondence. I too miss those long discussions we used to have back on campus.

All my love, always.

Martin